Full Bloom

Sally Handley

A Holly and Ivy Mystery

Printed in the United States of America

Cover Design: www.carolmonahandesign.com

First Printing, 20178

ISBN: 9781726865289

DEDICATION

TO

LUCKY

AMY

AND WINSTON (R.I.P.)

ACKNOWLEDGMENTS

As with my first two books, I'd like to thank my sister, Mary Ellen Handley, who is ever ready to visit stately homes and gardens with me and who helps me with all my medical research.

Secondly, I'd like to thank Nina Augello, my dear friend, who continues to amaze me with her willingness to read my chapters as I write them and who continues to be an inspiration for so much of whatever is good in the Holly and Ivy mystery series.

Thirdly, I once again want to express my special thanks to Steve Miller, proofreader non-pareil.

Thanks again to Carol Monahan, graphic artist extraordinaire, who consistently translates my ideas into images, and earns me countless compliments on my book covers. ww.carolmonahandesign.com)

I also owe a special debt of gratitude to my Cozy Mystery critique partners whose genuinely constructive critiques and suggestions have helped me in ways that cannot be measured:

- Judy Buch (www.judybuch.com/)
- Cindy Blackburn (cueballmysteries.com)
- Wayne Cameron, author of the Melvin Motorhead Series (available on Amazon)
- Diana Manley

Finally, thanks to Sisters in Crime (Sistersincrime.org), both the national and my Upstate South Carolina Chapter (sincupstatesc.blogspot.com) and Malice Domestic (malicedomestic.org). I appreciate the many kindred souls these organizations have linked me with, both published and unpublished writers, who constantly amaze me with their generosity of spirit and willingness to share their knowledge and experience.

1 KATE'S PLACE

"Remember what I told you before we left. I refuse to talk about it." Holly Donnelly slammed the car door leaving her sister Ivy sitting inside.

Ivy shook her head, pausing as she reached for the door handle. The two-hour drive from New Jersey to Kate Farmer's house in the Catskills had been deadly quiet. Since Ivy's arrival from South Carolina the day before, Holly had simply refused to discuss her break-up with Nick Manelli.

Ivy sighed and opened the passenger side door. By the time she got out of the car, Holly had opened the back door and Lucky, her border collie, jumped out. A smiling Kate Farmer appeared on the porch of the rambling Victorian house as her dog, Amy, bounded down the steps towards the newly arrived guests. Kate quickly followed, her arms open wide. She hugged Holly first, then Ivy as the dogs ran in frenzied circles around them, jumping up and down, barking wildly.

"Okay, okay, you guys. Calm down," Holly said reaching down to pet Amy.

"Don't waste your breath." The petite, olive-skinned Kate laughed, her cropped brown curls glistening in the sun. "This exuberance at the arrival of guests is a biological imperative. Actually, on the inside I'm feeling the same way." Kate put an arm around each of the sisters and squeezed. "It's so good to see you guys!"

"Good to see you, too." Holly smiled walking back to the car and opening the trunk. Amy and Lucky had calmed down, but the sound of barking continued, coming from the neighbor's yard.

"Who's that? Sounds like a big dog bark," Ivy said as she reached into the trunk and grabbed her overnight bag.

"Oh, that's just Winston, my neighbor Chuck's golden Lab. He and Amy share neighborhood watch duties. He'll calm down after we get out of the driveway."

"I hope so," Holly said. "Kate, could you grab my bag. I don't want to move again once I sit down on that porch. I'll carry the Michelob."

Kate eyed the case of beer and exchanged a quick glance with Ivy who just arched her eyebrows in reply.

****

"So what's new in Reddington Manor?" Holly asked after lunch as she dropped into a wicker chair on the side porch and poured beer into a frosted mug.

Kate's smile turned grim. "Believe it or not, quite a lot's been happening. And none of it good."

"Really?" Ivy sat forward, a look of alarm on her face.

"Really. There's been a rash of burglaries. Some people say it's drug dealers from Monticello." Kate frowned. "But a few people suspect Tommy Cranston and his friends."

"Cranston?" Holly wrinkled her brow. "Isn't that your neighbor's son? The one up the street."

"Yeah." Kate nodded. "But I don't believe it. Not Tommy."

"Do we need to be worried?" Ivy grimaced. "Aren't you afraid to be here all by yourself?"

Before Kate could respond, the barking next door resumed. "You hear that? Between Amy and Winston, I never worry. If you think this is loud, you should hear them if anything -- man or beast -- comes near our houses at night. Amy has an absolutely blood-curdling yowl she lets loose, and if Winston isn't already barking, she sets him off. That's when I relax and know I have nothing to worry about."

Holly laughed as she took another swallow of beer, but Ivy looked confused. "What do you mean?" she asked.

"Well, Chuck has what amounts to a small arsenal over there." Kate tilted her head in the direction of the ramshackle house next door.

"Oh." Ivy sat back, appearing a bit relieved.

"Yeah, I'd be more worried Chuck might accidentally start a fire and the whole place would explode like a powder keg." Holly chortled.

"Great." Ivy closed her eyes and shook her head.

"Stop scaring your sister. Let's change the topic to something more interesting," Kate said moving to the edge of her chair, focusing a penetrating stare at Holly. "Why did you and Nick break up, and what are you going to do to get him back is what I want to talk about."

Holly glared at her. "I told my sister before she got out of the car, and I'm going to tell you this only once. I have no intention of talking about it. We split up. End of story." She lifted the mug to her lips and finished what was left of her beer.

"Oh, come on!" Kate sat up straight and put her hands on her hips. "You've got to be kidding."

"No, I'm not." Holly stood up, grabbed her mug and the empty beer can and went inside the kitchen.

Kate looked at Ivy. "She's kidding, right?"

"No, I'm afraid not." Ivy shrugged. "She absolutely refuses to discuss it." Moving next to Kate on the wicker love seat, she whispered, "You know, I was ecstatic in January when she called to tell me Nick proposed."

"They seemed so happy and so perfect for each other." Kate shook her head, a perplexed look on her face. "Nick seemed like such a genuinely decent guy."

"I agree. I think the problem is Nick is as strong and sure of himself as she is."

Kate let out a sigh. "But that's why I thought, at 55, she'd finally met her match."

"Me, too."

"Shh. Here she comes."

Holly returned to the porch, another frosted mug and beer in hand. Dropping onto the cushioned chaise facing her friend and her sister, she smiled and said, "Lovely weather we're having, isn't it?"

"Holly!" Kate squealed, pounding the arm of the loveseat in exasperation.

"I'm sorry. I'm sure we can find plenty more interesting things to talk about." Slowly she poured the beer into the mug and the three women watched as the frothy head rose, stopping exactly at the top edge of the glass.

"This is going to be a mighty dull weekend if all we have to do is watch you pour beer into your glass," Kate muttered.

Holly grinned as she raised the mug in a toast. "Here's to a mighty dull weekend."

Before she could lower her glass, a loud and mournful howl pierced the air, causing her to spill some of the beer. Amy began barking and Lucky pointed her nose skyward and howled in reply.

"Lucky's never done that before," Holly said putting her mug down on the side table.

Kate stood up and looked toward her neighbor's house. "You know, Chuck's truck is in the driveway. He's usually gone to work before I get up, but I was so busy getting ready for your arrival, I didn't think anything of it." She started down the steps. "That dog's been barking off and on all morning. I wonder if something's wrong." She descended the steps and the dogs ran ahead in the direction of the howls. Holly followed.

"Wait." Ivy remained standing on the porch. "Why don't you call him first?"

Kate looked back and shook her head. "No. I'll just check on the dog."

Ivy sighed as she watched Kate, Holly and the two dogs disappear behind the stand of shrubs that partially separated the properties. After a moment she slowly walked down the steps and followed. The howling and barking stopped before she reached the shrubs.

Looking to her left, she saw Kate opening the gate of a huge dog pen at the far end of the property. Ivy laughed as a large yellow Lab jumped up putting its paws on Kate's shoulders, nearly knocking her over.

Turning towards the house, Ivy noticed the back door was ajar. She hoped Chuck wasn't loading his gun in response to the commotion in his backyard.

Cautiously, she approached the back stoop and stopped a few feet shy of the partially open screen door. "Hello." When no one answered, she repeated more loudly. "Hello. Anyone home?" Still no answer. Looking over her shoulder, she saw Kate was filling a water bowl from a hose and Holly was laughing as the three dogs cavorted on the grass.

Ivy turned and stepped on the cinderblock that served as a step to Chuck's back stoop. Again, she said, "Hello," as she leaned over and peered through the window. *Oh, no, no, no.*

On the floor a man was lying on his side. She felt an adrenalin rush as her nursing instincts kicked in. Pulling the screen door wide open she stepped inside. That's when she saw the meat cleaver in his chest. Dried blood surrounded the wound, darkening the red shirt he wore. A pool of blood trailed from the body under the refrigerator. Ivy's hand trembled as she felt for a pulse. Nothing.

Standing up, she turned and went back outside. Holly and Kate were headed towards her, laughing as Lucky rolled under Winston and knocked Amy off her feet.

"The poor thing was thirsty," Kate said. "He must have knocked over..." She stopped as soon as she saw Ivy's ashen face.

Holly ran to her sister. "What's wrong?"

Ivy sank down on the edge of the stoop. "It's not going to be a dull weekend."

2 SHERIFF CYRUS BASCOM

Kate sank onto the wicker loveseat and buried her face in her hands. Ivy gave her shoulder a comforting squeeze and Holly offered her the tissue box.

" I -- I can't believe it." Kate grabbed a tissue, dabbed at her eyes and blew her nose. "Maybe if I'd checked on him this morning..."

"Stop," Holly said dropping down on the loveseat beside her friend. "Don't even start thinking that way."

"That's right." Ivy nodded. "Judging by the wound and the amount of dried blood, I'd say Chuck was dead hours before you even woke up this morning."

Kate grabbed another tissue, shaking her head. "How could this have happened and I didn't hear a thing?"

Holly shrugged and looked across the yard to the house next door. Several State Police vehicles as well as the local sheriff's car filled the driveway and spilled onto the lawn. "Two policemen are headed this way," she said.

Kate followed Holly's gaze. "Oh, great. It's Sheriff Bascom and his deputy. He's the last person I want to talk to."

Before Holly could ask why, Amy and Winston sat up and began barking as Lucky issued a low growl.

Holly grabbed Lucky's collar. "Ivy, help me get these dogs inside, please."

Ivy jumped up and got hold of Amy and the sisters guided the dogs in through the kitchen door. They continued barking as Holly closed the door and she and Ivy returned to their positions on either side of Kate. All three watched as the middle-aged sheriff and a much younger deputy arrived at the foot of the porch steps.

The younger man remained standing in the yard as the paunchy sheriff swaggered up the steps, an air of self-importance accompanying him. He removed his hat revealing a glistening crewcut that, except for some graying patches, was probably the same look he sported in his high school yearbook picture.

"Ms. Farmer. Ladies. I'd like to ask you a few questions."

Kate sighed. "We already gave a statement to the State Police, Sheriff."

Bascom paused, twisting his mouth to one side. After a moment, he smiled and said, "Yes, I know, Ms. Farmer. Due to their superior forensics capabilities, the State Police will be assisting me in this investigation, but…"

"Assisting *you?*" Kate's expression registered disbelief.

The smile disappeared from Bascom's face and Holly noticed the deputy, who hadn't moved from his sentry post at the bottom of the steps, lowered his head slightly. She glanced back at the Sheriff whose expression had transformed into a malevolent glare.

"Yes, Ma'am. I'm still the Sheriff here in Reddington Manor and I have some questions the State Police didn't ask you."

Placing her hand on Kate's forearm, Holly glanced at Ivy who again gently squeezed Kate's shoulder. Kate sank back into the chair cushions. "Okay. What do you want to know?"

Bascom sniffed. "Did you see Tommy Cranston anywhere near Chuck's house yesterday?"

"Tommy? No. Why would you even ask me that?" Kate glowered back at her questioner.

"Well," the Sheriff drew the word out slowly. "You said you didn't hear anything during the night. Judging by the ruckus those dogs made when we headed over here, I think you would've heard something if a stranger came to the house last night." Smirking, he said. "I know Tommy sometimes took care of Chuck's animals."

Kate tried to sit forward, but Holly increased the pressure on her forearm. Glancing at Holly, she took a deep breath and replied, "No, Sheriff, I didn't see Tommy anywhere near Chuck's house yesterday."

"You're sure?"

Kate tensed and again tried to move forward. This time Ivy's hand on her shoulder stopped her. Stretching her neck forward, she raised her chin. "I'm sure."

The Sheriff's eyes narrowed as he stared at Kate. "Okay," he said, nodding as he looked down at the hat he slowly rotated in his hands. Looking back up, a grin returned to his face as he looked from Ivy to Holly.

"Ladies, pardon my manners. I'm Sheriff Bascom." He extended his hand to Ivy first, then Holly. "Are you twins?"

Holly stifled the urge to roll her eyes. "No. Just sisters."

"The resemblance is remarkable. Holly and Ivy Donnelly, right?" he asked. "Nice names."

"Why thank you, Sheriff," Ivy replied, tilting her head slightly. "Our mother was an avid gardener."

"My mother loved to garden, too." The Sheriff's grin broadened. "I'm very sorry we have to meet under these circumstances, but I'd still like to welcome you to Reddington Manor."

"Thank you," Holly said appearing amused at the shift in the Sheriff's demeanor from Bad Cop to Mr. Welcome Wagon in response to Ivy's Southern Belle charm.

"The State Troopers told me you arrived from New Jersey today. What a pity this happened on your first day in our town. Will you be here long?"

"Depends on the weather," Holly replied.

"Is that right?" Bascom again looked down and shook his head. When he looked back up, he wore a pained expression on his face. "Well, I certainly wouldn't want anything to happen to you," he said looking from Holly to Kate. Turning to Ivy his expression softened. "But you don't have to worry about a thing. I'll have increased patrols up and down this street until we catch this killer, which I don't think will take long. You see anything suspicious, you call me."

Returning his hat to his head, Bascom headed down the steps, chuckling as he said, "I know Ms. Farmer has the number."

3 THREES

"I hate him!" Kate pounded both fists on the kitchen island counter, causing the dogs to scatter.

Holly sighed. "Okay, calm down. And lower your voice -- unless you want us to close all the windows and doors."

Kate pursed her lips and headed into the living room. She sank onto her recliner as Holly and Ivy sat down on the couch. The dogs stood watching and once the women appeared settled, they each found a spot on the floor.

"Okay," Holly began. "Besides the fact that Sheriff Bascom is a pompous, good ole boy, why do you hate him?"

"First of all, did you see how he asked me about Tommy? He's already decided Tommy did this. The only investigating he's going to do is looking for evidence that points to him."

"Why did he laugh when he said you had his number?" Ivy asked.

Kate grimaced, then looked down at her hands folded in her lap. “Over the years, I may have made a call or two to the Sheriff's office.”

Holly exchanged a look with Ivy. “Give us a for instance.”

“Well,” Kate sighed and paused. After a moment, she looked up. “Last month I called him a few times about what's been going on next door.”

“Out with it, Kate,” Holly said.

“I don't think you ever met my neighbor, Milly Leggett. She's a lovely woman and has been a great neighbor. About two months ago she had a bad fall down her basement steps. She's only seventy-five, but she had to have a hip replacement followed by weeks of therapy.”

“A lot of seniors don't survive long after they break a hip,” Ivy said. “Any word on whether or not she's coming home?”

“That's just it. I don't know. Last month her son Boyd showed up one day. When I asked him, he said she's still at a rehab facility.” Kate frowned. “That's when he started coming around every weekend with a bunch of low-lifes in tow.” Moving to the edge of her chair, she said, “The electricity and water are turned off, so they were outside all Saturday and Sunday. And when they weren't drinking and blasting music, they were burning toxic-smelling stuff in the back yard.”

“And so you called the Sheriff about them,” Holly concluded.

“Yes, and he did nothing but come over here and tell me how men sometimes just need to blow off steam and that burning trash isn't against the law in Reddington Manor.”

Ivy scratched her head. “This Sheriff doesn’t seem to like ‘low-lifes’. Why do you think he didn’t do anything about the neighbor’s son?”

“I can only guess it’s because I’m still considered an outsider here compared to the Leggetts.” Kate replied. “You know most people still call this place the Molly Goldstein House. She’s the woman I bought it from twenty years ago.”

“Really? Holly said, a surprised look on her face.

“Oh, I get that.” Ivy nodded. “I’ve lived in the South for thirty years, and I’m still considered a Yankee. And let’s not forget that you’re a woman by yourself.”

“Yeah, there’s that.” Kate leaned her head on the back of her chair and looked up at the ceiling.

“Why does Bascom have it in for Tommy?” Holly asked.

Kate sat forward again, her brow wrinkled. “That’s a good question. You know, I’m not sure.”

“You seem pretty sure Tommy didn’t kill Chuck,” Ivy said.

“Look.” Kate moved to the edge of her chair. “Tommy used to hang out with us when my kids were little. He’s done some jobs for me. I’m telling you, he’s a really gentle soul. Just because he got into some trouble when he was thirteen...” She broke off and leaned back into the cushions.

“What happened?” Ivy asked.

“He and a couple of other boys stole some things from the dollar store. But it was Chuck who bailed him out and took him under his wing. Even if I thought he was capable of killing someone -- which I don’t -- he’d never kill Chuck.”

“Where’s his father?” Holly asked.

"Nobody knows who his father is," Kate frowned. "Raquelle, his mother, is kind of the town floozy. She got pregnant in high school and, as far as I know, she never told anyone who Tommy's father is."

"Small towns, big secrets," Ivy mused, looking out the window. After a moment, she stood up, "Hey, what do you say we go out to dinner? My treat."

"I think that's a great idea," Holly agreed.

Kate shrugged. "I don't have much of an appetite."

"Then you can have a glass of wine." Holly smiled. "You know I always say you don't drink enough."

****

As they waited for Kate in the kitchen, Ivy refilled the dogs' three water bowls. "I think I'm not coming to visit you anymore," she whispered.

Holly blanched, looking as if she'd been slapped. "Why would you say such a thing?"

"Because every time I've visited you in the past year, someone has died."

Holly shook her head and frowned. "Oh, don't be ridiculous. People die every day. This is just a bizarre coincidence."

"Call it what you want. All I know is three visits, three deaths."

"Hey, don't they say these things happen in threes? After this one, we're good."

"I hope you're right," Ivy said arching both eyebrows.

Holly grinned. "I'm always right."

4 FLO DWYER

Kate nearly spilled her wine as she roared with laughter. Holly just frowned.

Ivy slapped the table and leaned toward Kate. "I know. Can you believe it? She actually said she's always right!"

Holly sipped her beer and looked across the restaurant as her sister and friend continued giggling. "Are you finished?" she finally asked as the giggles subsided.

"Oh, c'mon," Kate said. "That's the first laugh I've had all day."

"Yeah," Ivy said. "Lighten up. I knew getting out was exactly what Kate needed."

Holly sighed, an indulgent smile on her face. "Glad to be the source of your comic relief."

"You have to admit, saying you're always right is particularly funny after Lyla Powell's murder," Kate chuckled.

"And," Ivy added, "I'm sure whatever happened between you and Nick, you were not right."

"Oh, no, you didn't," Kate muttered, placing her elbow on the table, covering her eyes with her hand.

After a few moments of silence, she peeked through her fingers at the two sisters locked in a glaring contest.

Finally, Holly put her glass down and slid out of the booth. Placing her hands flat on the table, she leaned towards Ivy. “I don’t care what you say, sister dear, I’m not talking about it.” Standing up straight, she sniffed, “Now if you’ll excuse me, I’m going to the ladies room.”

As she disappeared through the doorway marked “Restrooms”, Kate turned to Ivy. “I can’t believe you said that!”

Ivy gave her head a weary shake. “That time she was right. I was baiting her. I know it sounded mean, but I really just wanted to get her talking. If she didn’t respond to what I said just now, I guess she’s never going to tell us what happened.”

“I was so sorry when she told me about the split up.” Kate leaned back and took another sip of wine. “I really feel bad for her.”

“Oh, me too,” Ivy sighed. “But I can’t help wondering if she wasn’t the cause of the breakup. She’s been masterful at self-sabotage since her breakup with Brian.”

Kate’s eyes widened, then darted to the restroom doorway. “Shh. Here she comes.”

Holly smiled serenely as she slid back into the booth alongside Ivy. She’d just picked up her glass when the restaurant entrance door opened.

“Oh, wow,” Kate whispered. “That’s Chuck’s wife.”

The woman stopped just inside the doorway and surveyed the room. A faded pastel blouse served as a jacket over a white polyester shell that hugged her plus-size frame. Her baggy blue denim pants were frayed at the hem that dragged behind her Birkenstock sandals. Her graying hair, cut in a bob, looked as if it hadn't been combed. When she spotted Kate, she waved and lumbered over to their table.

"Flo, I'm so sorry…" Kate began.

"Yeah, yeah, yeah." Flo waved her hand in a dismissive motion. "I heard you were the one who found him."

Kate nodded. "These are my friends, Holly and Ivy Donnelly. Actually, Ivy is the one who found Chuck."

The big woman cast a glance at Ivy and nodded. "Good thing. The Sheriff said he'd only been dead a few hours. Any longer and he'd a really stunk up the place. As it is, I can't get in until Bascom says it's okay."

Kate hesitated, fidgeting in her seat. After an uncomfortable silence she asked, "You have a place to stay?"

"Oh, yeah. I checked myself into the Robin Hood Inn," she chuckled. "Nobody to stop me from spending Chuck's money now."

Kate picked up her wine glass and took a long swallow.

Holly looked from Kate to Flo. "They notified you pretty quickly," she said.

"Yeah, I was still Chuck's emergency phone number. Dumbbell." Flo smirked and shook her head.

Holly picked up her glass and chugged what was left. Ivy started to say something, stopped and just lowered her head.

From behind the bar, the waitress held up a small shopping bag. "Your take-out's ready."

“That’s me.” Flo looked down at Kate. “Thanks for saving me a trip to the morgue to identify the body.” Turning to Ivy, she sneered, “And thanks for saving me the trouble of finding a smelly corpse.”

The three women watched her walk away. After she’d exited the restaurant, Ivy shivered, “What an awful person!”

Kate slowly shook her head from side to side. “I never really liked her, but I didn’t think she was this cold and heartless. Poor Chuck.”

“Were they separated?” Holly asked.

“No. They had this weird on-again-off-again relationship. Whenever they had a fight, she’d go stay with her sister. I haven’t seen her in a few days, so I guess that’s where she was the night Chuck was murdered.”

The trio sat silently until the waitress came by. “Anybody need anything?”

“Another round, please,” Holly said. Neither Ivy nor Kate objected.

****

The sun had nearly set as Holly pulled into Kate’s driveway. They could hear Amy barking as soon as they opened the car doors.

“Let’s get these puppies walked,” Holly said. “After that, I’m going straight to bed.”

“Me too,” Ivy said. “I’m exhausted.”

“Me three.” Kate unlocked the door. “Don’t forget we have the Trout Parade tomorrow.”

“Oh, my gosh,” Ivy said, “With everything going on, I completely forgot about the parade.”

After walking the dogs, Holly and Ivy waited in the kitchen as Kate locked up. “Should we move furniture in front of the doors?” Kate asked.

Holly smiled. “I don’t think anyone will get past these dogs tonight.”

“They did last night,” Kate said.

“Yes, but Lucky wasn’t here then. Everyone’s a stranger to her.”

Ivy sighed. “I wish Nick were here.”

Without a word, Holly turned and headed upstairs.

5 MOVING ON

Nick pulled Holly close and kissed her -- one of those slow, sensuous kisses that left her in a languorous muddle.

“Stop,” she said, pulling back.

“What’s wrong?” he asked, shaking his head.

“You always do this.” She tried to break loose, but he wasn’t letting go.

“Do what?”

“You start kissing me when I’m trying to make a point.”

Nick laughed.

“It’s not funny. You know that’s what you do.” She continued to struggle against Nick’s grip. “Let go of me.”

Holly wakened with a start. She couldn’t move. Tangled in her bedsheets she needed to roll over to get free. Sitting up, she realized she’d been dreaming about Nick. It wasn’t the first time. She was sure all the pressure from Ivy and Kate to talk about their break-up caused her to dream about him tonight.

Reaching to the nightstand, she felt around and finally put her hand on her cellphone. 3:34 AM. This was not good. If she didn't fall back to sleep, she'd be a zombie by noon.

When would these dreams end? She hated them. They always felt so real. Or was that just her memory playing tricks on her? One night she actually thought she smelled his aftershave.

Putting the phone on the nightstand, she lay back down nestling into the pillows. She had to forget him -- move on, as they say. They were simply incompatible in so many ways. Turning on her side, she sighed. But they were compatible in some very important ways.

Ugh! She tossed on her other side. The dreams about his kissing her were always the worst. She'd actually feel his lips on her neck -- her ear -- her lips. She stretched and curled her toes, flipping on her back, staring at the ceiling in the dark.

Maybe she should just get up and try to read. Propping herself up on her elbow, she again reached over to the nightstand feeling for her Kindle. She had to stretch a bit to reach it. As she did, she glanced out the window towards the Leggett house. A brief beam of light in a second-floor window caught her eye. How could that be? Didn't Kate say the electricity over there was shut off? Sitting up she fixed her eyes on the window. Nothing. *Just my imagination.*

Leaning back, she turned on the Kindle. Looking at the opening screen, she shook her head. Fat chance Judy Buch's murder mystery, *Venom*, was going to put her to sleep. Returning to her home page, she tapped on this month's book club selection, Ali Smith's *How to Be Both.* If that didn't get her to nod off, nothing would.

6 THE TROUT PARADE

"Here comes the Trout Man!" Ivy pointed past the Dairy Fairy Float to a man wearing a rubber trout head waving to the crowd.

"Only in Reddington Manor!" Holly laughed.

"That's right," Kate chuckled. "Where else could you see an entire town shut down to celebrate the humble trout?"

"Speaking of trout, I'm hungry," Ivy said, looking at her watch.

"Yes, I think it's time for refreshment," Kate nodded. "Let's head to the Trout and Bear Pub before the parade finishes and we have to stand in line for an hour."

The three women wove their way through the crowd filling the sidewalks, arriving at the rustic gates bearing a coat of arms with a smiling trout and a growling grizzly.

"Oh, this is lovely. All these picnic tables out front remind me of those English pubs," Ivy said.

A young woman wearing a bib apron with a smiling trout stenciled on it came over. "Would you like to sit outside or inside?" she asked cheerfully.

Kate looked at the two sisters. "Outside," Holly and Ivy said simultaneously.

The hostess grabbed three menus and led them to a table midway between the entrance gate and the restaurant.

"Perfect," Kate said as they sat down.

"Your server will be with you in a moment," the hostess said.

The trio immediately fell to perusing their menus.

"What kinds of desserts do they have?" Ivy asked turning over her menu.

"I think they have tiramisu and gelato," Kate replied.

Ivy's face lit up. "I'm in heaven."

"Can I get you ladies something to drink?"

All three women looked up at a tall, platinum blonde woman, also wearing an apron with the ubiquitous smiling trout. The apron hugged her curves and her blouse was unbuttoned to reveal her ample décolletage.

"Hi, Raquelle," Kate said. "I didn't realize you worked here."

"I just help out on busy weekends," she said without smiling.

After taking the drink order, the buxom waitress headed back to the restaurant, when a voice called out."Hey, Raquelle, honey, c'mere."

A hulk of a man in a Buffalo Bills t-shirt waved her over to a seating area positioned outside to the left of the restaurant building. Seated on Adirondack chairs that circled a firepit, he and his friends all grinned in Raquelle's direction. The curvy blonde stopped, smiled and slowly walked over. An interchange between her and the hulk took place. The entire group burst into loud laughter. She cast a playful grin over her shoulder, as she sauntered back into the restaurant.

"I'll bet she does very well on tips," Holly said, a droll expression on her face.

"Yeah," Kate chuckled. "I'm sure she does." Leaning forward she whispered, "That's Tommy Cranston's mother."

"The boy the Sheriff blames for Chuck's murder?" Ivy asked.

"Yep." Kate sighed.

In just a few minutes Raquelle returned with the drink order.

"You heard about Chuck?" Kate asked.

Raquelle's eyes narrowed as she shot a grim-faced glance at Kate. "Hard not to." She pulled out her note pad and asked, "Ready to order?"

"Yes, I'll have the trout special," Holly replied.

"Me, too," Ivy added.

"Make it three." Kate handed Raquelle her menu.

After she walked away, Holly grimaced. "Awkward."

Kate leaned in. "I'm sure the Sheriff has been to see her. I just want her to know I don't think Tommy had anything to do with Chuck's murder."

"Maybe you should just say that," Ivy suggested.

A look of uncertainty on her face, Kate hesitated, then finally nodded. "You're right. I'll wait until we get the check."

Kate made no further attempt to talk to Raquelle as she served the meal and replenished their drinks. After Ivy finished her tiramisu, the waitress stopped at the table and asked, "Anything else?"

"No, just the check," Holly replied.

When she returned, Kate looked up. "Raquelle, the sheriff asked me if I'd seen Tommy around the day of Chuck's murder. I told him absolutely not. I want you to know that I don't think for one minute Tommy had anything to do with it."

Raquelle stiffened and stared coldly at Kate. "That's not what Bascom said."

Kate's eyes widened. Before she could respond, Holly did. "Then he's lying. My sister and I were with Kate when he questioned her and we had to actually hold her down when he asked her about Tommy."

Kate shook her head. "Raquelle, I know your son and I know he'd never hurt Chuck."

Raquelle's stance softened. Under her breath, she said, "I should have known that bast… Bascom was lying."

"Is there anything I can do?" Kate asked.

Raquelle bit her lower lip, then shook her head. "Don't worry about Tommy and me. We can take care of ourselves." She put the check down on the table and walked away.

"Can you believe that Bascom? Why would he lie like that?" Kate banged both fists on the table.

Holly frowned. "Cops -- even good cops -- lie if they think it will help their investigation." Before Kate or Ivy could reply she reached for the check, stood up and said, "Let's go."

7 BOYD LEGGETT

Sunday morning Holly followed the aroma of freshly brewed coffee downstairs.

"Good morning," she said as she entered the kitchen. She froze in the doorway as Kate turned to her with a look of distress on her face. "What's wrong?"

Kate held up the milk pitcher. "I used up the milk in the pancake batter and now there's none for coffee."

Holly laughed. "Relax. Is the supermarket open this early?"

"Yeah, they actually open extra early on Sunday to sell newspapers."

Holly grabbed her handbag and car keys. "I'll just run downtown and get a gallon of milk. Do you need anything else?"

"Maybe a dozen eggs," Kate parted the café curtain and looked out the window towards Chuck's house. "I was counting on getting them from the chickens next door, but now I'm afraid to cross that yellow police tape." Letting go of the curtain, she turned back to Holly and frowned. "I'd call downtown to see if I could at least go over and tend to the hens, but I'm not sure I could control myself if I had to talk to Cyrus Bascom." Kate leaned over the sink and spit right after saying his name

"Let me guess. Your Italian grandmother used to do that."

"Yeah." Kate nodded. "Nothing expresses utter disdain better than spitting."

. "In that case, I definitely think it's best you avoid any contact with Bascom."

Kate narrowed her eyes and peered out the bay window facing the back of her property. "You know, I could cross over to Chuck's yard behind the barn. They didn't tape all the way to there." She smiled and snapped her fingers. "That's what I'll do. Forget the eggs."

"You're sure?" Holly asked, with a skeptical raise of her eyebrow.

"Yep. Those chickens need food and water." Kate grabbed a basket from the counter. "Besides, if you don't collect the eggs, they'll actually stop laying."

"Really? You learn something new every day." Holly chuckled as she opened the door and stepped out on the porch, Kate right behind her.

Lucky, Winston and Amy who'd been lying on the porch, got up.

"No, no." Kate said. "You stay. I'll be right back."

Amy let out a frustrated whine, but all three dogs remained on the porch and watched as Kate headed to the back of the yard and Holly got in her car and drove off.

Crossing into Chuck's yard behind the barn, Kate entered the "coop complex", as Chuck used to call it. She carefully latched the pen gate behind her. First, she collected eggs in her basket. "Not bad, girls," she said aloud after she counted ten eggs. Finally, she spread chicken feed and refilled the water tins.

Kate gave one last look around, then opened the gate and re-latched it behind her. Midway across the lawn, she heard Lucky's bark. She looked to the driveway and saw Boyd Leggett out in the road. When he spotted her, he started up the drive, but Lucky jumped off the porch and charged at the scruffy-looking man.

"Lucky," Kate shouted, running after her, Amy and Winston bringing up the rear. Boyd stopped and stood still as Lucky circled around him, sniffing.

"New dog?" he asked.

"No. She's my friend's," Kate replied as she reached Boyd and grabbed hold of Lucky's collar.

Amy and Winston approached Boyd who bent and extended a downturned hand. "Yeah, you guys know me. Tell your friend I'm a good guy."

Kate grimaced slightly. As Boyd returned to an upright position, she said, "Let me get this dog inside. I'll be right back. C'mon, Lucky."

Reluctantly, the dog accompanied Kate, struggling to look over her shoulder at Boyd, apparently unwilling to turn her back on him. Kate put the egg basket down at the bottom of the steps and tugged on Lucky's collar to get her up the steps. Once the dog was inside, she quickly closed the door and turned back to see Boyd standing at the bottom of the stairs eyeing the eggs. He looked as if he hadn't shaved in a week and his black hair, though combed, hadn't been washed in some time.

"How's your mother?" Kate asked.

"Not real good," he replied. "We're prob'ly gonna have to put the house up for sale. That's why I stopped by. Got to start getting the place ready. I packed a few things in my truck just now." He raised his chin in the direction of the driveway next door.

"I'm sorry to hear that. Please give your mother my regards."

"I will. I know she always liked you," Boyd said looking from her to the egg basket.

"Do you have a phone number where I can reach you?" Kate asked. "If I hear of anyone who's looking for a place, I'll let you know."

"Oh -- well -- I just lost my cellphone," Boyd replied, not making eye contact. "And, anyway, we're nowheres near ready to show the place."

Kate started down the steps. "You going to use a realtor?"

Boyd backed up a few steps. Rubbing the bristly stubble on his chin, his eyes remained fixed on the eggs. "I don't know. I guess so." His eyes darted quickly to Kate, then back to the basket. "Hey, could you spare me a couple a those eggs?"

Kate's eyes widened just a bit. "Sure," she said. "Let me get a bag from the kitchen." Lifting the basket, she went up the steps. She had to hold Lucky back as she opened the door. Grabbing a paper bag from the counter, she placed five eggs inside.

Boyd was standing staring at Chuck's house when she came back outside.

"Shame about Chuck, isn't it?" he said, turning back towards her.

"Yes. Yes, it is," she replied, handing him the bag.

"Sheriff Bascom says he thinks Tommy Cranston did it." Boyd's eyes narrowed as he looked at Kate.

Kate simply stared back at him. He quickly averted his eyes. "Says he's convinced it's Tommy 'cuz he hasn't been able to find him since it happened."

Kate crossed her arms in front of her. "Well, I hadn't seen Tommy for a several days before Chuck was killed, and I live on this street, so my guess would be Tommy wasn't even in town the night of the murder."

Looking at his feet, Boyd nodded. "Yeah, you're prob'ly right. Well, thanks for the eggs." He turned toward the driveway, then stopped. Still avoiding eye contact, he said, "I won't be back for another week or so. Can't stay over 'cause -- well, you know -- the gas and electric's shut off. Water, too."

Kate struggled to conceal the glee she felt hearing she would have at least seven Boyd-free days to look forward to. "Thanks for letting me know. I'll keep an eye on the place."

Boyd's head shot up and a look of alarm crossed his swarthy face. "Oh, no need for that. Really nothin' a value in there." His concerned expression transformed to a smirk. "Thieves'd actually do me a favor if they emptied the place. Save me the trouble, huh?" He turned and walked to the driveway, tossing a wave over his shoulder. "See ya round."

Kate watched as Boyd reached the end of the driveway and turned up the hill to his mother's house. Shaking her head, she mounted the steps and went inside heading straight upstairs. The bathroom door was closed. Quickly, she scurried to her bedroom, opened the closet door and grabbed a pair of binoculars from the top shelf. When she stepped back into the hall, the bathroom door opened.

"Good morning," Ivy said smiling.

"Good morning," Kate replied, brushing past her. "Sorry, but I'm in a hurry."

Kate ran into the room Holly was using and went straight to the window.

"What's wrong?" Ivy asked. "Where's Holly?"

Kate raised the binoculars to her eyes. "Nothing's wrong. Holly just went to the store."

"What are you looking at?" Ivy peered over Kate's shoulder into the neighbor's yard. "Is that the guy you told us about? The one you called the police on?"

"Yes." Suddenly Kate gasped as Boyd Leggett got in his truck and backed out of the driveway.

"What is it?" Ivy asked.

Kate lowered the binoculars. "That tarp he covered the truck bed with--that's Chuck's tarp."

8 FLO RETURNS

Holly slid her last piece of pancake through a pool of maple syrup. "But how can you be sure it was Chuck's tarp?" she asked.

Kate pounded the table with her fist. "Because it had paint spatters on it that match the paint in my laundry room. That's the tarp Chuck used when he patched a wall crack for me."

Holly leaned back in her chair and sighed. "So what do you want to do?"

"Call the State Police," Kate replied.

"Not Bascom?" Ivy asked.

Kate jumped up. "How could you ask me that? I just told you what Boyd said about Bascom. I will not talk to that lying sack of…"

"Calm down, Kate," Holly soothed.

"I won't calm down." Kate started pacing. "I can't calm down. How can I calm down when I now know Boyd Leggett killed Chuck?"

Ivy bit her lower lip as she glanced at Holly, a beleaguered expression on her face. After a moment, Holly patted Kate's chair. "Please sit down. Remember how you were the voice of reason during the Lyla Powell case? Let's talk this through before you do something that could make matters worse. Please."

Kate stopped pacing, closed her eyes, and dropped her shoulders. After a moment she returned to the table and sank into her chair.

"Nobody knows how you feel better than I do," Holly began. "But let's just discuss what could happen if you call the State Police instead of Bascom."

"Yes," Ivy nodded. "A man like Bascom won't like your going around him."

"So?" Kate asked, a flash of belligerence in her eyes.

"Well, my late husband, Dave, used to say, 'Don't make enemies you don't need to'."

Kate huffed. "Bascom's already my enemy."

Ivy tossed an exasperated glance at Holly.

"Okay," Holly intervened. "Let's say you're right. What are you going to tell the State Police? That Boyd has Chuck's tarp? Even if you could prove it's Chuck's tarp, it's not exactly evidence Boyd killed him."

"I hate to say this." Ivy put her hand on Kate's. "It's not even proof Boyd stole the tarp. He could say Chuck gave it to him."

"And you know that's exactly what Bascom will say," Holly added.

Kate dropped her head. "Dammit. You're right." When she raised her face, her eyes glistened. "What am I going to do?"

Ivy sighed. "I have a suggestion Holly won't like." Sitting back she locked eyes with her sister. "Let's call Nick and ask him for advice."

Wearily, Holly shook her head. “Not gonna happen in this life.”

“Then what?” Kate squeezed her hands into fists.

The three women sat silently, each lost in her own thoughts. Their contemplating was interrupted after a few minutes when the dogs began barking. Holly walked to the door. “Looks like the mountain’s come to Mohammed.”

Kate and Ivy followed Holly to the window in time to see a boxy gray Kia Soul pull into Chuck’s driveway followed by a police cruiser. Flo Dwyer slowly got out of the Kia and Sheriff Bascom and the young deputy who’d accompanied him on Friday got out of the cruiser. The deputy started to remove the yellow police tape.

Kate backed away from the window and started to the door. “Excuse me.”

The two sisters turned to face her, blocking her exit.

“Are you serious?” Kate asked. “You’re not going to let me out?”

“We’ll let you out,” Holly said. “Just promise you’ll stay calm.”

Kate inhaled deeply then exhaled slowly and smiled. “I’m calm.”

Holly opened the door and Ivy put her hand on Kate’s shoulder. The three women stepped out onto the porch where the dogs sat, all eyes focused on the neighboring driveway.

“Ready?” Holly asked, glancing sideways at Kate.

“Ready,” Kate replied.

The trio of women descended the steps, the dogs bounding past them as they walked across the yard.

"Good morning," Kate said.

"Morning," Sheriff Bascom replied, touching the tip of his hat.

Flo frowned and gave a half-hearted wave. "I see you have Chuck's mutt."

"Oh," Kate said, looking down at Winston. "Yeah. We've been looking after him. I guess you'll want him home with you now."

"Hell, no," the big woman sneered. "You want him? He's yours."

As if he understood the words, Winston looked up at Kate, awaiting her reply. "Of course, I'll keep him if you don't want him." Seeming reassured, the dog sat down, his butt partially on Kate's foot.

"Good," Flo said, looking up at the roof of the house. "One less thing I need to get rid of."

Kate grimaced. "Uh, Sheriff. Something happened this morning that I-- um -- I'd just like to let you know."

"What's that, Ms. Farmer?" the sheriff asked squinting

"Boyd Leggett stopped by. He said they were going to be putting his mother's house up for sale and he was packing up some things."

"Doesn't surprise me. I'd heard Milly wasn't doing so well." A smile twitching at the corners of his mouth, Bascom said, "Well, it looks like your problems with Boyd and his friends will be over then, doesn't it?"

"Yes, that's right," Kate said. "It's just that as Boyd was driving away, I noticed the tarp he covered his truck bed with was a tarp that, I'm sure, belonged to Chuck."

Sheriff Bascom sighed. "Now, how could you be sure of that?"

Kate bit the corner of her mouth and Holly moved closer. "Well, you see, Chuck did some work for me last month and he used that tarp and spilled some paint on it. I recognize the splatter."

The lawman let out a soft chuckle. "Recognize the splatter, huh? So what are you saying? Now you accusing Boyd of murdering Chuck?" His expression turned menacing.

Before Kate could reply, Flo turned around and faced Bascom. "Maybe he did and maybe Tommy did. I don't care who killed Chuck. What I care about is my property. If I know Boyd, he stole that tarp and who knows what else from this place."

Holly, Ivy and Kate watched in silence as the sheriff's menacing glare softened a bit. "Flo, you don't know Boyd stole that tarp. Maybe Chuck gave it to him."

"Boyd?" Flo scoffed. "Not likely. Chuck couldn't stand him. Said he was a worthless piece a…"

"Now, Flo…"

"Don't you 'now Flo' me, Cyrus. If that bum thinks he can come around here and steal stuff just because Chuck's gone, he's got another think coming. You better track him down and warn him, I'll put a hole in him just as soon as look at him. And you know I will."

The sheriff nodded, licked his lips and looked over in the direction of his deputy. "You done there, Jason?" he shouted.

"I mean it, Cyrus." Flo glared. "No jury's going to convict a widow who shoots a trespasser -- especially after her husband was murdered in his own kitchen."

The sheriff nodded. "I'll talk to him." He walked to his car, got in and turned on the ignition. The deputy, his hand full of yellow tape, jogged from the back yard and got in the passenger side.

As they drove off, Kate smiled. "So, Flo, are you moving back in?"

"Oh, hell no! I wouldn't stay another night in this dump," she said giving a magician's assistant arm sweep toward the house. "No, I'm just gonna take a look around -- see what's worth selling. Get Chuck's bank and insurance information. Tomorrow I'll come back with a friend a mine whose daughter's good with computers. We'll see what we can get rid of on Craig's List."

"That's smart," Kate said. "Let me know if there's anything I can do."

"Uh-huh," Flo said, opening her car door and grabbing her handbag.

Holly and Ivy had already started back across the lawn to Kate's house. Kate began to follow, stopped and turned back to face Chuck's widow.

"Flo, I almost forgot. I came over this morning and fed the chickens and collected some eggs. You want me to keep doing that? Shall I save you the eggs."

Flo snorted. "Well, I sure as hell don't plan on tending chickens, and I'm enjoying my eggs cooked sunnyside up courtesy of the Robin Hood Inn. You want to tend those chickens, be my guest. In fact, if you want 'em, get somebody to move that coop over to your place. Otherwise, those hens are gonna be fricasseed." Cackling, she went inside and left Kate standing in the driveway, both her eyes and mouth wide open.

9 A GAME OF CLUE

Kate entered the kitchen as Holly was pouring another mug of coffee. Shaking her head, she said, "Unbelievable. I don't understand how Flo can be so -- so…"

"Heartless?" Ivy offered.

"Exactly."

"What did you go back to tell her?" Holly asked.

"I wanted to know if I should look after the chickens. I won't even tell you what she said, but essentially, the coop and the hens are mine for the taking."

"I was kind of amazed at how she talked to Bascom," Ivy said.

"Me, too." Kate's brow furrowed. "I sure didn't know they were on a first name basis."

"And he took her seriously," Holly added. "When he talked to you he was patronizing, but not with her."

"What do you think their relationship is?" Ivy mused, "They're about the same age. Do you think they had a thing in the past?"

Kate shrugged. “I don’t know. I guess that’s possible.”

“Or maybe they just grew up together. In a small town there’s a lot of ways they could be connected.” Holly rinsed out the empty coffee carafe. “You want me to put on another pot?”

“No.” Kate shook her head. “More caffeine will just make me want to jump out of my skin.” She stood quietly staring at the floor. After a moment she looked up grinning. “What do you say to a game of clue?”

Holly groaned.

“C’mon.” Ivy stood up. “This always helps us.”

“No, it doesn’t,” Holly countered. “It never helps. It didn’t help when we tried to figure out who killed Edna Hagel and it didn’t help when we tried to figure out who murdered Lyla Powell. We just spin our wheels and go nowhere.”

“Maybe,” Kate said standing up. “But spinning wheels serve a purpose, too.”

“You mean besides wasting gas and burning rubber?” Holly smirked

Kate waggled her head at Holly. “Spinning wheels weave yarn.” Smiling smugly, she headed upstairs. “I’ll get pads and pens.”

Settled in the living room, Kate began. “To start, we need a list of suspects.”

“Then means, motive and opportunity.” Ivy clicked her ballpoint pen and started writing.

“This is nuts.” Holly stared at the blank page. “We don’t need these legal pads. There’s only two suspects, Tommy Cranston and Boyd Leggett.”

“What about the nebulous drug dealers from Monticello?” Kate asked.

"The dogs would have raised holy hell if strangers had broken in and killed Chuck. Even I have to agree with Bascom on that point," Holly said.

"I hate to ask this, but wouldn't they have done the same thing if Boyd came around at night?" Ivy asked.

Kate looked up at the ceiling, wrinkling her brow. Sitting forward, she shook her head, "No. No they wouldn't. This morning only Lucky growled and barked when Boyd started up the driveway. Winston and Amy know Boyd." A satisfied smile on her face, she jotted on her pad. "Boyd definitely is a suspect."

Holly twirled her pen. "So we have two suspects."

"Wait a second," Ivy said. "What about Flo?"

"Wow!" Kate dropped her pad and stared at Ivy. "You're right. The dogs wouldn't have barked at her."

"I know she seems rather unfazed by Chuck's death, but would she actually put a meat cleaver in his chest?" Holly asked.

"Yeah," Ivy nodded. "That's such a crime of passion. She seems -- well -- rather dispassionate."

Kate sighed. "I don't know. I honestly don't. But it definitely is a possibility. If anyone had a motive to kill Chuck, she sure did." She sank back in her chair and jotted something on her legal pad.

"Okay, anyone else at all you can think of who could get past the dogs?" Ivy asked.

"Not that I know of," Kate replied.

Holly tapped her pad with her pen. "So these three suspects all could have had opportunity. We don't know if any of them has an alibi. And the cleaver was in the kitchen, so whoever got in had the means. What about motive?"

"Well, I don't think Tommy had a motive, that's for sure," Kate said.

"Then why has he disappeared?" Holly shot Kate a penetrating glance.

"Can you blame him?" Kate pounded the side of her chair with a clenched fist. "Bascom's got his sights set on him. What else could he do?"

"It does make him look guilty," Ivy grimaced apologetically.

Kate shook her head from side to side, jutting out her chin. "He has no motive."

"But Flo definitely does. And maybe Chuck caught Boyd stealing."

Ivy sighed, "But Bascom would argue the same about Tommy."

Holly threw her pad on the coffee table. "What's the point of this? I mean, no matter what, there's nothing we can do."

Kate leaned her head on the back of her chair and sighed. "I guess you're right. There is no point."

"Okay, then," Ivy said, laying her pad and pen down. "Kate, didn't you say there's a diner in Jacksonville that serves homemade pies?" Holly and Kate exchanged a glance, turned and stared at her silently.

"What?" Ivy said, bending her arms at the elbow and turning her hands palms up. "We have to eat."

10 NIGHT VISITORS

Ferocious barking pierced the night air. Holly jumped up in bed, her heart pounding. Lucky ran out of the bedroom, her nails clicking as she flew down the back stairs. Holly glanced at the clock. 2:24 AM. She pulled on her sneakers and dashed out into the hall just in time to hear footsteps descending the staircase.

"Kate!" she called out, but received no answer.

Ivy came out of her room, clutching her robe. "What's going on?"

"Don't know, but it can't be good." Holly headed down the steps, Ivy right behind her.

The kitchen light was on and the back door open. The sisters scurried out on the porch just in time to see Kate walking up the driveway, a broom slung over her shoulder. In the glow of the porch light they could see the three dogs feverishly sniffing around Chuck's house.

"Are you crazy?" Holly asked. "You ran out here in the dark by yourself with a broom for protection?"

Kate shrugged. "The dogs were with me."

"Oh, Kate!" Ivy grabbed her by the arm. "A man was killed here two nights ago. What were you thinking?"

Kate lowered her head. "I guess I wasn't." Looking back up, she smiled. "The good news is we scared off whoever it was."

"C'mon." Holly shook her head grabbing Kate by the other arm. "Let's get back inside." She turned and whistled. Lucky, Amy and Winston came running.

In the kitchen, Holly glared at Kate as she took the broom from her and propped it against the wall. "Call the police."

Kate sank in a chair and frowned. "Is that really necessary?"

Ivy grabbed the phone. "I'll do it," she said and dialed 911.

As Ivy placed the call, Holly turned to Kate. "Did you see anyone?"

"No. As soon as I flipped on the porch light, I heard an engine start. The dogs flew out the door in front of me and by the time I got to the end of the driveway, all I saw were red tail lights turning the corner at the bottom of the hill."

Ivy hung up. "They said they'll send someone over." Sitting down beside Kate, she exhaled loudly. "I still can't believe you went out there."

"Well, what was I supposed to do?" Kate asked, a sheepish expression on her face.

Ivy shook her head. "Flip on the lights, let the dogs out and call the police. That's what."

"It could have just been a wild animal," Kate said. "Up here you don't call the police every time your dogs bark."

"Oh, that's just great!" Holly stretched her neck forward. "And the broom would have been a big help against a bear or a mountain lion."

Before Kate could reply, Lucky growled and went to the door at the sound of a car coming up the driveway, Amy and Winston following. Holly peered out the window. "You're in luck. The deputy's by himself."

Kate got up and opened the door. The dogs ran out and circled the young policeman, who stood still and let them sniff. "It's okay," Kate called to the dogs. "C'mon in, Jason."

Inside the kitchen, the deputy removed his hat.

"I don't think you met my friends when you were here the other day -- Holly and Ivy Donnelly. This is Officer Jason Bascom," Kate said making brief eye contact with Holly as she said the deputy's last name.

Nodding at the sisters, the policeman asked, "What happened?"

Kate recounted the events of the evening starting with the barking dogs, ending with the tail lights.

Looking out the window towards Chuck's house, the deputy said, "No lights on over there. That's a problem. We'll call Mrs. Dwyer tomorrow and recommend she leave some lights on." Turning back to Kate, he continued. "In the meantime, Ms. Farmer, I suggest you call us if the dogs raise a fuss. Don't go outside by yourself."

Holly and Ivy both turned and smiled at Kate. Suddenly, the dogs started to bark at the sound of another vehicle coming up the drive. Officer Bascom turned to look through the screen. Gently, he pushed the dogs away from the door and stepped outside.

Holly went to the window. “It’s the sheriff.”

Kate and Ivy watched from the door as the sheriff, not in uniform, stood talking to the younger Bascom.

“Is the deputy Bascom’s son?” Holly asked.

“His nephew,” Kate replied.

“Uh-oh. Here he comes.” Holly moved away from the window.

“Ms. Farmer, may I come in?” the sheriff asked through the screen.

Kate stood up. “Of course.”

Stepping inside, the elder Bascom nodded at Holly and Ivy. “Evening, ladies.” Turning to Kate, he said, “Jason told me what happened. Says you didn’t get to see the vehicle.”

“That’s right,” Kate replied. “Just tail lights.”

The older man sighed and bit his lip. “Still no sign of Tommy Cranston?”

Kate stared at him for a moment, her jawline twitching. “No,” she finally replied, the single word chilling the room.

“Just asking,” the sheriff said, lowering his gaze.

Kate raised her chin. “Did you talk to Boyd Leggett like Flo asked?”

It was the sheriff’s turn to stare at Kate. “No,” he returned icily.

“Sheriff,” Holly intervened, breaking up the staring duel. “The other day you said that Tommy could have gotten into Chuck’s without the dogs’ barking. Tonight the dogs went wild when whoever it was pulled up next door."

"Oh, yes, Sheriff." Ivy nodded, smiling warmly at him. "They scared us half to death. We're glad Officer Bascom came so quickly." Standing up she said, "We're sorry to get you out in the middle of the night. Can I put on some coffee?"

The sheriff's icy coating melted under Ivy's gaze. "Kind of you to offer, Ms. Donnelly, but no thank you. Wouldn't want to put you to any trouble." Turning back to Kate, his smile faded, but his expression had relaxed. "We'll talk to Flo tomorrow about how to secure her place. In the meantime, you do like Jason said. Those dogs raise hell, you call us and stay inside. I don't need another crime scene to investigate."

Kate just nodded.

Bascom turned and opened the door. Over his shoulder, he said, "Lock this door behind me."

Holly closed the inner door and turned the bolt lock. Grabbing the broom, she turned grinning. "So glad you didn't argue that you were armed."

"Very funny." Kate sneered.

"Don't tease, Holly," Ivy admonished. "But really, Kate, I agree. No more running out into the night."

Kate's shoulders sagged. "I guess that was stupid. Thank you both for stepping in when things got a little tense there." Laughing, she looked at Holly. "I enjoyed it when you used Bascom's own argument about the dogs' barking to shoot down his Tommy Cranston theory." Tilting her head to the side, she said, "I know I didn't see anybody out there before, but I feel pretty sure it was Boyd."

Holly sighed. "The only problem is the dogs didn't bark at Boyd earlier today. If it was him, why did they bark tonight?"

"Oh, yeah." Kate frowned.

"Well, if he was accompanied by someone the dogs didn't know, they'd bark, wouldn't they?" Ivy offered.

"That's right," Kate straightened up.

"But the same can be said about Tommy then," Holly countered.

Kate shook her head. "I'm going to bed. I just can't think about this anymore."

As they heard Kate mount the stairs, Holly turned to Ivy. "Listen, I think..."

"Yes," Ivy said.

"What are you saying 'yes' to? I haven't even asked anything yet."

Ivy smiled. "You think we should not go home tomorrow -- that we should stay here until they catch whoever murdered Chuck. You were going to ask me, if that's okay with me. Right?"

"Right." Holly nodded and the two headed upstairs to bed.

11 BENNY

"Good morning." Holly raised her coffee mug in a toast as she stepped out onto the porch. "Looks like it's going to be a beautiful day."

"For you maybe." Kate frowned, looking up from the newspaper. You're going home."

Holly grinned. "Oh, that's right. We didn't get to tell you last night. We decided to stay a few more days -- if that's alright with you."

Kate's eyes widened. "Are you kidding? Of course, that's alright with me. I'd be happy if you two stayed the rest of the summer."

Holly just smiled, sank down into the cushions of the loveseat and took a sip of coffee.

"I can't tell you what a relief this is." Kate folded the paper and leaned back in her chair. "I felt rather fearless running outside last night, but when I woke up this morning I realized how foolhardy that was. Then I remembered you and Ivy were leaving today and..."

"You really didn't think we'd leave you here alone -- especially after last night."

Kate groaned. "Ivy's going to hate me. I'm sure you guys had plans for this week."

"Relax. Ivy's the one who suggested it before I even asked."

"Suggested what?" Ivy asked through the screen door.

"I just told Kate we're staying."

"Of course." Ivy opened the door, balancing a dessert plate bearing a blueberry muffin on top of her mug. "Is that Flo's car?" she asked looking out to the road, where a grey Kia was approaching.

"Yep, that's her," Kate replied.

Flo's Kia spit gravel as it climbed the drive. The car came to a halt and the two doors on the passenger side opened. A woman with tightly-permed grey hair and a much younger woman got out. Flo's door opened and she hoisted herself out of the car. Looking towards the porch she waved and all three women headed across Kate's lawn.

"I heard you girls had some excitement last night," Flo chuckled as she mounted the porch steps.

Kate wrinkled her nose "Excitement is not the word I'd use, but I guess you could say that."

Flo smirked, then pointed with her thumb to the woman beside her. "This is my friend, Barbara and her daughter, Ashley. She's the computer whiz." Dressed in Daisy Duke denim shorts, her brown, curly hair tied up in a high ponytail, Ashley smiled and waved. Barbara just nodded.

"Nice to meet you," Kate said. "These are my friends, Holly and Ivy."

"Are you twins?" Ashley asked.

Holly shook her head and Ivy replied, laughing, "No, just sisters."

"Don't they look alike, Ma?" Barbara again just nodded in reply.

"Enough with the chit-chat," Flo cut in. "We got to get started over there." Flo raised her chin in the direction of the house next door. "There's a boatload of stuff to go through. You know, Chuck could never throw anything away." She shook her head then turned back to Kate. "Don't worry about a repeat of last night. I'm working on something."

"Such as?" Kate asked.

Grabbing the bannister rail Flo started down the steps, "I called my sister to see if her son Benny will stay over. I'll let you know what he says."

"Okay." Kate said. She watched as the three women crossed the lawn and entered the house.

"Do you know this Benny?" Holly asked.

Kate grimaced and shook her head.

Ivy picked up her muffin, staring at it appreciatively. "Anybody in the house is better than nobody."

"I agree." Holly nodded.

"We'll see." Kate pursed her lips. "We'll see."

****

"Gin!" Ivy grinned as she laid down her cards.

"That makes three games in a row." Kate threw her hand down in disgust. "Great!" she said as one of the cards blew off the table and out into the yard.

"I warned you. She's a card shark." Holly said tapping the screen of her Kindle. She snuggled into the chaise cushions as Kate scurried across the porch and down the steps to retrieve the card.

As Kate returned to the porch, Lucky sat up and growled. The sound of an engine grew louder and both Winston and Amy stood up and stared out to the road. All three dogs began to bark as a gleaming black Chevrolet Silverado pulled into the driveway next door.

Kate turned and called to the dogs. "It's okay. It's okay."

The dogs stopped barking, but stood on alert as a tall, young man with his black hair tied in a man-bun got out of the driver side and waved. Chains linked to his leather belt jangled as he moved. A leather vest topped a white T-shirt, revealing arms completely covered in tattoos.

Kate waved back as the passenger-side door opened. A much larger man got out of the car, his caramel-color, bald head glistening in the sunlight. When he turned, Kate bit her lip to keep from gasping. The left side of his face was covered in a tattoo designed to look like an eye patch. Kate smiled lamely as the two men headed to the back door of Chuck's house.

"C'mon, you three." Kate called to the dogs and mounted the steps. She stood silently, facing Holly and Ivy, her wide eyes unblinking.

"Benny?" Holly grimaced.

Kate just lowered her head in reply, her shoulders sagging.

12 TOLD YOU SO

"Don't jump to conclusions," Ivy said as Kate sank onto a wicker chair. "Remember, you can't judge a book by its cover."

"Besides," Holly added, a droll expression on her face, "their appearance alone may be enough to keep looters at bay."

Kate glared at Holly. "Very funny."

"Oh, come on," Holly snickered. "Tell me you don't think this is amusing."

"We'll see how amusing you think this is tonight when we can't get any sleep because our new neighbors invite a few friends over."

"That could be fun," Holly said, fighting back a belly laugh.

"Stop it," Ivy said. "You're not helping." She turned to Kate. "I'm serious about not judging these guys until you meet them. Once when I was driving, I ended up in a ditch trying to go around a car that was broken down." She moved to the edge of her seat. "Two scary looking men on motorcycles stopped and got my car back on the road in no time. Before I could reach in my handbag to get some money to give them, they were back on their bikes, driving down the road." Ivy gazed dreamily across the yard at the truck parked next door. "I guess you could call that a life-altering experience."

"You never told me about that," Holly said.

Ivy sniffed. “You think you’re the only one who can keep things to herself?”

“Here we go again,” Kate said, sighing and shaking her head.

“Sorry. This isn’t about us.” Holly faced Kate. “Seriously, though, just wait and see. After all, that may not even be Benny. That might just be two guys who came over to buy something.”

Next door the sound of a screen door slamming caused all three women to look in that direction. Flo and the two men were headed across the lawn. Kate stood up to greet them as the dogs jumped off the porch and surrounded the approaching threesome. The fellow sporting the man-bun bent down. “Hiya, Winston. How you doin’, boy?”

Amy stood watching. Lucky came up behind the man with the eye-patch tattoo. He stood still as she sniffed and moved in front of him. Slowly, he lowered his upturned hand. She licked it, looked up at him, then turned and walked back to the porch.

Reaching the bottom of the porch steps, Flo tilted her head and pointed with her thumb. “Kate, this is Benny. He and his friend here are going to be staying over for a couple a nights.”

Benny stepped forward and extended his hand. “Hi, Kate. Aunt Flo told us what happened last night.”

He smiled as he shook her hand. “Don’t you worry. Me and Razor here, we won’t let nothin’ happen.”

Kate forced a smile, glancing from Benny to the somber Razor, who gave a slight nod of affirmation. “Well -- uh --that’s reassuring,” she said. “Oh. These are my friends Holly and Ivy. They’ll be here with me a few nights, too.”

"Okay, then. I just didn't want you to come out later and attack these guys with a broom." Flo snorted as she turned and headed back across the lawn.

Benny grinned. "Yeah, we heard about that. Like I said, you don't need to worry. We're gonna nip this thing in the butt, right, Razor?"

"In the *bud*, Benny," Razor said softly, turning to follow Flo.

"Yeah, yeah," Benny replied, waving off Razor's revision. "He's always correctin' me, but this time, I really mean in the 'butt'." Benny winked at Kate.

"Let's go, Benny," Flo shouted over her shoulder. "We got work to do."

A grinning Benny gave a mock salute and trotted off behind Razor.

When they disappeared inside, Ivy stood up, a smug expression on her face. "Told you so."

13 RAQUELLE

An afternoon of catnaps, dog walks and gin rummy passed uneventfully. As Kate prepared dinner and Holly and Ivy set the table, the phone rang.

"I'll get it," Kate hollered as she came inside carrying a bowl full of lettuce she'd picked from the side garden. "Hello."

The sisters entered the kitchen, their eyes on Kate.

"Uh huh." Kate nodded. "Yeah, sure. We're just about to have dinner, but we can stop by when we walk the dogs -- in about an hour."

Kate hung up the phone. "That was Raquelle."

"Something wrong?" Holly asked.

Kate frowned. "I think so."

"Has Tommy been arrested?" Ivy asked.

"I don't know." Kate frowned as she put the lettuce bowl on the counter and turned off the burner under the pot of boiling pasta. "All she said was that she needed to talk to me."

****

Raquelle opened the door and stepped out onto her porch. Her eyes were red as she looked from Kate to Holly and Ivy.

"You remember my friends?" Kate said. "They can take the dogs home if you want to talk to me alone."

Raquelle shook her head, sank onto the glider, and buried her head in her hands. Kate handed Amy's leash to Holly, walked over and sat down beside the distraught woman. "What's wrong?" She put her hand on Raquelle's shoulder. "Has something happened to Tommy?"

Raquelle sat up, her eyes red and glassy. "That's just it. I don't know, and I don't know what to do." She again lowered her head.

Kate shrugged slightly, making eye contact with Holly who'd remained standing in the yard with Ivy and the dogs. "When's the last time you saw Tommy?"

Raquelle wiped the tears from her face. "The day Chuck was murdered."

Kate sat still, slowly exhaled. "Uh -- I'm not sure what I can..."

"Me, either," Raquelle said, her expression hardening. "All I know is you said you didn't think Tommy did it."

"And I don't." Kate put her hand on Raquelle's arm. "If I can help, I will."

The young woman bit her lip as she studied Kate's face. "Okay," she sniffed, seeming resolved and continued. "They asked me to work at the restaurant Friday night, so I went straight there from my day job. That's where I heard about Chuck.

Tommy came by and told me his friends said Bascom was looking for him." She stared over the porch railing into a copse of trees, her jawline pulsing.

Kate again looked over at Holly and Ivy. Holly nodded slightly and Ivy gave her a reassuring smile and sat down on the bottom porch step.

"Then what?" Kate asked.

Raquelle turned back to Kate. "I gave Tommy all the cash I had and told him to go stay with a friend of mine in Monticello. I talked to him Saturday and Sunday, but I couldn't reach him today. I called my friend and he said Tommy never got there." She moved to the edge of the glider. "I don't know where he's been the last two days and I don't know where he is now."

"Oh, boy." Kate lowered her head, staring at the porch floorboards.

"What about his friends?" Holly asked.

"I called them. All their phones went straight to voicemail."

"Maybe that's a good sign," Ivy said. "Maybe they're all together."

The sound of a classic I-phone ringtone interrupted the discussion. Raquelle jumped up and ran inside.

"This isn't good." Kate looked from Holly to Ivy.

"No," Holly agreed.

"It does make him look guilty." Ivy grimaced.

"Worst of all," Kate shook her head, "Raquelle can't go to the police for help finding him."

Kate got up and walked to the door. She turned her head, straining to hear. After a moment, she whispered, “I can't hear anything.”

Holly's eyes narrowed. “Do you have any idea where he might be?”

Kate gave a slight nod. “I may…”

The screen door flew open. Raquelle's swollen eyes blazed. “I'm going to kill him myself when I get my hands on him.” She paced to the end of the porch and back. “That was Tommy's stupid friend, Hank. He said Tommy's safe and hiding some place.” Clenching her fists, she snarled. “He swore he didn't know where Tommy was -- that Tommy said everyone was safer if they didn't know.”

“Well, at least you know he's okay,” Kate said.

Raquelle's rage appeared to evaporate as she once again dropped onto the glider and began sobbing.

Kate sat down and gave Raquelle's back a reassuring pat. “Look, Tommy's no dummy. I don't like this either, but we don't have any choice. We have to trust him. Wherever he is, he's safe from Bascom.”

“Damn Bascom!” Raquelle punched her thighs with clenched fists. “Why didn't I just sleep with the old bastard?” Her shoulders sagged and she lowered her head.

Kate's eyes widened. “Is that why he's always been out to get Tommy? Because you wouldn't sleep with him?”

Without lifting her head, Raquelle just nodded.

Kate's chin jutted forward as she squeezed Raquelle's shoulder. "I'll help you."

"How?" Raquelle croaked.

"I don't know right now, but I promise I will."

Holly and Ivy said nothing as they exchange a telling glance.

14 TAROT

After saying goodbye to Raquelle, Kate ran down the porch steps and started speed-walking down the street, Amy trotting beside her.

"This isn't good, is it?" Ivy said as Winston tugged on the leash she was holding, forcing her to pick up her pace.

"No," Holly answered. She and Lucky also quickened their steps. "We better hurry before she gets inside the house and calls the sheriff's office."

Out of breath, Holly and Ivy entered the house. Amy greeted them, but Kate was nowhere in sight. "At least she's not on the phone." Holly hung Lucky's leash on the wall hook and went to the living room. "Kate," she called up the stairs.

"Just a minute," Kate hollered. "I'll be right there."

The sisters dropped onto the sofa. Kate bustled down the stairs, a canvas bag in her arms. She sank down on her recliner and started rummaging in the bag, finally extracting a deck of Tarot cards.

"Oh!" Ivy started giggling. "That's a relief."

"What do you mean?" Kate looked confused.

"I don't know." Ivy gave a sheepish shrug. "You really despise Bascom, and the way you took off from Raquelle's, I wouldn't have been surprised if you had pulled a gun out and suggested we become vigilantes."

Kate jerked her head back and frowned. "You know me better than that," she said. "Or maybe you don't."

"Hey, if I didn't know that was your Tarot bag," Holly said, "I might have been a little worried, too. The way you flew down the street, I wasn't sure what you were planning to do."

"Seriously?" Kate sneered at Holly. "You don't know by now that the first thing I do when I'm upset or confused is consult the Tarot cards?"

"Sorry," Ivy intervened. "You're right. Even I should know that by now."

"Okay, then." Kate took out the deck and knelt in front of the coffee table. Shuffling the cards, she laid them out in a Celtic Cross spread, plus four cards underneath. No one said a word as she slowly turned over the cards in the basic 10-card spread.

"Well?" Ivy asked edging forward. "What's it saying?"

Kate grabbed her notes. "The heart of the matter is the Ace of Wands, which is a positive card." Rifling through her pages, she finally stopped. "It's a card of creation. Ah, but also a card of family, origin, birth."

"You think this might have something to do with whoever Tommy's father is?" Holly asked.

Kate pursed her lips. "I don't know." Squinting, she looked at her notes again. "This card could also refer to money, fortune or inheritance."

"Maybe Chuck left a will." Ivy said. Her eyes widened. "You don't think he could be Tommy's father, do you?"

Kate shook her head. "No way."

"But you said Chuck mentored Tommy," Holly said. "If there is a will, do you think he left Tommy something?"

Kate studied the card. After a moment she said, "I guess that's possible."

Ivy sighed. "Unfortunately, that's a motive for murder."

Holly jutted her chin in the direction of the cards on the table. "Keep going."

Looking down at the spread, Kate continued. "Okay. The Ace of Wands is crossed by the Moon--a card of illusion, lies and deception. Over here we have The Seven of Swords. That card shows a guy getting away with something -- could be theft."

"He reminds me of someone," Ivy said. After a moment she snapped her fingers. "I know. He looks like Boyd, doesn't he?"

Kate gave Ivy an admiring glance. "He does. And for sure Boyd's always trying to get away with something."

"Let me see." Holly sat forward. "Wish I'd been here when he stopped by." She pointed at the Ten of Swords. "I don't think you need to look this one up."

They sat staring at the picture on the card -- a body face down with ten swords in its back.

Kate sank down on the floor, lowered her head and put her notes to the side. “Poor Chuck.” After a moment, she sat up, her eyes glistening. “You know, I forgot to ask Flo about a funeral.”

“You honestly think that harridan is going to have a funeral for him?” Holly asked.

“She doesn’t impress me as the grieving spouse -- more the merry widow,” Ivy said, “though there’s nothing particularly merry about her either.”

“Well, we’ll see about that.” Kate got back on her knees, a determined look on her face. “Tomorrow, I’m going to talk to her about it. People in this town respected Chuck. She has to do something.”

Holly pointed at the cards. “Finish the reading.”

“Well, we know the Tower is all about destruction. And over here we’ve got the Eight of Swords -- a woman bound and blindfolded, surrounded by swords, and the Nine of Swords, a woman crying underneath nine swords hanging over her. Either one could be Raquelle.”

“As long as neither one is you,” Holly said.

Kate didn’t look at Holly. Instead she put her finger on the outcome card. “Well, here’s The Seven of Wands. Look. It’s a young man brandishing a wand. He’s under attack. That’s got to be Tommy.” Kate shook her head. “I don’t like this. He’s got to fight to hold his ground.”

“By going into hiding, that’s what he’s trying to do,” Holly said.

“You forgot this one.” Ivy pointed at the Devil card.

Kate smirked. “Clearly, that’s Cyrus Bascom. What a pig he is!”

“Well, now we know why he’s out to nail Tommy. This takes sexual harassment to a whole new low,” Holly said.

Ivy frowned and looked back down at the spread on the table. “What are those four cards there?”

“Oh,” Kate said starting to turn them over. “These are what’s underneath it all. Oh, my! These are fabulous. First we’ve got the Three and Ten of Cups.”

“They all look so joyful,” Ivy said. “Are we those three women holding up the cups?”

“I sure hope so,” Kate giggled. “That card is so clearly about a successful conclusion, a celebration. And the ten is a card about marriage and domestic happiness. And who do we have here?” Kate looked up smiling at Holly.

Holly got up abruptly and headed upstairs. “I’m going to bed. See you in the morning.”

“What just happened?” Ivy asked as Holly disappeared up the stairs.

“The Empress here,” Kate pointed, grinning, “has to be Holly. And in all my readings for the past year -- since before she even admitted she’d met him,“ Kate pointed at the next card, “the King of Wands has always been Nick.”

“Oh,” Ivy sighed. After a moment her eyes lit up as they came to rest on the happy couple with their arms around each other standing below the ten golden cups arched across a rainbow.

15 FIREWORKS

After brushing her teeth, Holly returned to her bedroom and closed the door. Sitting down on the bed she reached for her phone. No voice messages. Only spam in her email. A lump formed in her throat as she turned off the phone.

She'd become addicted to a daily call from Nick in just the few months they'd been together. Even when he was wrapped up in a demanding investigation, he always remembered to call her. No matter what.

Should she call him? No, no. It was over. They simply weren't compatible. End of story.

She got into bed and willed herself to go to sleep. After only a moment, she opened her eyes and stared at the ceiling. What a mess! This visit was supposed to be a relaxing vacation. What had they gotten themselves into? Was staying a mistake? But how could they leave Kate here alone?

They couldn't. Especially after last night. She punched her pillow remembering Ivy's words of the other night.

"I wish Nick were here."

Of course, Nick would know what to do. She remembered when he'd moved in with her and Ivy during the Lyla Powell investigation. She never felt safer than when he was in the house.

Yeah, maybe they'd be safer if he were here, but he'd only tell them to leave the detective work to the police and stay out of it. Maybe that was what they needed to do. But leaving things up to Sheriff Cyrus Bascom didn't give her the same re-assuring feeling leaving things up to Detective Nick Manellli had.

Of course, she didn't trust Nick when she first met him either. She was certain he was a racist cretin when he'd arrested her landscaper, Juan Alvarez, for the murder of Edna Hagel. She'd been very wrong about that. Still, she didn't think Cyrus Bascom was going to turn out to be a gruff old guy with a heart of gold. Not after what Raquelle told them.

Flipping on her back, she again closed her eyes. And again, after just a moment, her eyes popped back open and she sat up straight. Were they in danger? She really hadn't thought much about that. She'd put her sister in harm's way in the past, and she didn't intend to repeat that mistake. Suddenly, she remembered Benny and Razor. Smiling, she lay back down. They seemed like nice guys, and she actually did feel safer knowing they were next door.

Why did this have to happen while she and Ivy were visiting? How long would they have to stay? Grunting, she tossed on her other side. Maybe they could talk Kate into returning to New Jersey with them. She could stay until they found Chuck's murderer. Yeah, that could work. First thing tomorrow she'd suggest it.

She closed her eyes again. This time the image of a weeping Raquelle made her sigh. Kate had promised to help her. Holly doubted she could convince Kate to abandon Tommy and his mother.

Kate was so sure Tommy was innocent of killing Chuck, but she could be wrong. Holly knew what it was like to have a blind spot for someone you cared about. Still, even though he ran away, he could be innocent. Holly understood his thinking that his mother and friends were safer this way. But where was he? Surely, someone had to know where he was hiding.

Wait a minute! She had asked Kate if she knew where he could be. Kate had started to answer, but stopped when Raquelle came back out on the porch after the phone call from Tommy's friend.

But wasn't there something else she was supposed to ask Kate? Flipping on her side, she looked out the window. The stars were brilliant in the clear, night sky. Just like they were on Valentine's Day at Skyview Manor. She remembered Nick coming up behind her and resting his chin on her shoulder as she gazed upward. "Almost like fireworks," he'd whispered in her ear.

Holly sat up. "No, no, no," she muttered to herself. "I will not think about him. I will not call him."

She sank back down onto her pillow and gazed out the window toward the abandoned Leggett house. Suddenly, she saw a brief flash of light in the upstairs window next door. *That was not my imagination. Now, I remember. That's what I was supposed to ask Kate about.*

She got out of bed and walked over to the window. Was someone in the Leggett house right now? Was it Boyd? Or was it whoever interrupted their sleep last night? She stood watching for a few minutes, but the light did not reappear. Maybe it was just a reflection of light from the neighbor's house on the other side of the Leggett's.

Dropping back into bed she wondered if Boyd had anything to do with Chuck's murder. Had he hidden in the house, waiting until the middle of the night to sneak out and go over to Chuck's house and kill him? But why? Nobody mentioned anything being stolen -- except for the paint-stained drop cloth Kate saw covering Boyd's truck.

Holly laughed to herself. She hated to admit that Bascom might be right this time. Maybe Kate's dislike of Boyd and her suspicious nature had gotten the best of her. After all, it was unlikely that anyone would kill for a used drop cloth. But was anything hidden under that drop cloth?

Turning away from the window, Holly closed her eyes and said a prayer. *Please -- send us no nocturnal visitors, neither flesh and blood felons, nor phantom lovers.*

Finally she drifted off to sleep, but then jerked herself awake when she dreamt of Benny lighting a match and Razor asking her if she wanted them to start the fireworks.

16 THE CHICKEN COOP

"You look awful," Ivy said, as she came from the laundry room into the kitchen, a roll of duct tape in her hand.

"Thanks." Holly frowned and poured herself a cup of coffee. "What's going on out there?

"Benny and Razor are helping us move the chicken coop. When you finish your coffee, come help us."

"I think I'll just watch." Holly smiled and took a sip from the mug she'd just filled.

"What's wrong?" Ivy asked, a look of alarm on her face. "Don't you feel well?"

"I had trouble falling asleep, that's all. I think I just dozed off when the hammering started."

Ivy looked at her askance.

"I'm fine." Holly made a shooing motion. "Go. I'll be out in a minute."

Ivy shrugged and headed outside. Holly downed her coffee and followed. She got outside just in time to see Ivy disappear around the side of the garage. Picking up her pace, she started to jog across the lawn. Just as she reached the property line, she had to stop.

"Coming through," Benny shouted.

Holly backed up as Benny and Razor came from around the garage, dragging a hen-house on wheels as if it were a giant pull-toy. Lucky, Amy and Winston ran alongside, Kate behind them.

"Okay, that's where I want it." She pointed to the far corner of the yard.

Benny's pants chain jangled as he and Razor made a 90-degree turn and continued dragging the coop to the spot Kate indicated.

Ivy smiled as she came up alongside Holly. "These guys are great. They dismantled the fencing from the coop without any trouble. I thought they'd need their truck to pull the coop, but they said no, and they were right."

"Razor looks like he could pull the whole house. Do these two have jobs?"

"I asked them about that. They're sort of free-lancers. They do odd jobs for people."

"And they can make a living doing that?" Holly looked skeptical.

"Yeah." Ivy nodded. "Think about it. If you needed to move a chicken coop, who would you call? There must be hundreds of jobs like that up here."

"Enough to pay the rent and keep a truck like that Silverado on the road?"

"Well, Benny told me they live in an apartment over a barn at a farmhouse about ten miles from here. A New York City couple owns it. They only come up now and then, so Benny and Razor take care of the place and live there rent free."

"Amazing," Holly said as she watched Kate and the unlikely duo reach the back of the yard.

"Yeah. Kate says with all the people who've bought weekend and summer places up here, these guys are in high demand. Hey, where are you going?" Ivy asked as Holly turned and headed back to the house.

"With those two on the job, you certainly don't need me. I'm going to get another cup of coffee and watch from the porch."

In no time, Benny and Razor positioned and leveled the coop. Holly sat on a wicker chair watching in amusement as Kate, Ivy and their two, new best friends carried fence posts and chicken wire from Chuck's yard to the new coop site. After another half hour of digging and hammering, the job was complete. The foursome crossed back into Chuck's yard.

When Ivy re-appeared, she called out, "Holly! Come here. You have to see this."

Holly reluctantly got up and walked across the yard just as Razor came around the garage. Walking slowly, he held his massive hands out in front of him, above the reach of the dogs who circled around him, their noses turned upward. Holly approached cautiously. Her apprehension faded as she saw the yellow heads of four small chicks nestled in Razor's hands.

"Oooh!" she cooed. "They're adorable."

"Aren't they?" Ivy said as Razor continued to carry his precious cargo to their new location. "Hey, could you get the dogs in the house until we're done bringing all the chickens over?"

"Sure," Holly said, as she called the dogs. All three looked at her, then back at Razor. Reaching into her pocket, she found some leftover dog treats from their walk the night before. "Look what I have." Lucky knew what those words meant and came running. Amy and Winston hesitated just a moment, then raced after her.

Inside, Holly gave each of the dogs a treat and refilled the water bowls. As she stepped back out onto the porch, she saw an unsmiling Ivy racing towards her.

"What's the matter?" Holly asked

"Benny sliced his hand with a saw blade. I need to get alcohol and towels."

Holly waited on the porch as Ivy went inside to collect what she needed. When she returned, they jogged across the yard, reaching Chuck's back stoop just ahead of Kate, Benny and Razor. Holly hopped up onto the stoop and held the door open. Razor had Benny's hand in a vice-like grip as he guided his friend inside. Blood covered both their hands.

"Straight to the sink," Ivy called as she followed them.

Kate shook her head. "I can't believe this happened. Just when everything was going so well."

"What exactly happened?" Holly asked.

"He reached for a tool hanging on the pegboard and a saw blade slipped and did a number on his hand."

Holly grimaced and the two women stepped inside. They watched as Ivy used the kitchen sink sprayer to rinse the blood off Razor's and Benny's hands.

"That's right, Razor," Ivy said. "Keep the pressure on for a few more minutes."

"Will I need stitches?" Benny asked, his face pale.

"We'll see," Ivy replied. "Razor's quick response may have saved you from a trip to the emergency room." She slid a chair over from the table. "Here. Sit down."

"I'll check the medicine cabinet." Kate crossed the kitchen to a small bathroom. Returning, she said, "No bandages or gauze in there. Just Band-aids."

"Yeah, they won't do." Ivy shook her head. "We'll use the towels to bandage the cut." Ivy looked at Benny. "Okay. We're going to have to pour alcohol on the cut and it's going to burn."

Benny swallowed hard. "I know. We have to kill any microorgasms, right?"

Razor lowered his head and sighed. "Microorganisms, Benny. Microorganisms."

17 TWO QUESTIONS

Holly stepped onto the porch with a frosted mug and beer can, a wide grin on her face. Ivy started to giggle. Kate lowered the book she was trying to read and covered her mouth with her hand, stifling a laugh.

Holly sat down on the loveseat beside Ivy and whispered. “Have you ever had a microorgasm?” She quickly covered her mouth to muffle her chuckles.

“How would you…” Ivy chortled, “how would you know?”

Giggling softly, Kate scratched the back of her neck. “Remember Thumbelina?”

Ivy nearly spilled her tea and Holly slid off her chair to the floor, using both hands to cover her mouth as all three women started laughing uncontrollably.

When the giggles finally subsided, Kate sighed as she dabbed at her eyes with a tissue. “We have to stop this.”

“We could go inside, shut the windows and doors and howl until we really get it out of our systems,” Holly suggested as she cracked open her beer and poured it into the mug.

"You have to admit, Razor and Benny are nothing like what you expected, Kate." Ivy smiled.

"That I will admit," Kate replied.

"Hey," Ivy sat forward. "Before I forget, what was the name of that plant you put on Benny's cut. Razor's application of pressure to the cut was the best first aid, but that plant sure helped stop the bleeding completely."

"Oh, that." Kate got up, and walked out to the garden where she picked a plant. Returning to the porch she handed the plant to Ivy. "This is yarrow. You just dry the leaves and crumble them into a powder."

"Seriously?" Ivy stared at the plant in her hand. "How did you learn that?"

"Oh, I've always been interested in natural herbal remedies," Kate replied. "I've taken a few classes and done some research." She looked over at Holly. "You know -- for that book I'm not writing."

Ivy's brow wrinkled. "A book you're *not* writing?"

"Yeah, how's that going? Have you written anything?" Holly smirked.

Kate let out a deep sigh. "Well, I'm still working the story out in my head."

Holly glanced at Ivy. "That's why we refer to it as the book she's *not* writing."

"What's the book about?" Ivy asked.

"Well, it's a dystopian story about a time when people have to go back to relying on herbal remedies and living without electricity."

Holly snapped her fingers and moved to the edge of her seat. "That's it. With all the excitement around here this morning, I forgot I had two questions to ask you."

"Questions about what?" Kate asked.

"Didn't you say the electricity was off next door?"

"Yeah. That's what Boyd said."

"Well, I woke up around 3:30 the night we got here and thought I saw a light next door."

"Three thirty in the morning?" Ivy shook her head. "Sure you didn't imagine it?"

Holly sighed. "That's exactly what I thought, but last night I could swear I saw it again."

Kate shrugged. "I don't know. Boyd said he wouldn't be back much because everything -- power, water, gas -- was shut off. Could it just have been a car light reflection?"

"I guess," Holly replied. "I thought maybe it was a light from the neighbor on the other side."

"I hope it's not some squatter who discovered the place is abandoned," Ivy said.

Kate grimaced. "I doubt it. I haven't seen any strangers around. I haven't even seen any cars I don't recognize come up or down the street this week -- especially since the police are patrolling -- since Chuck's..."

Holly and Ivy sat silently as Kate lowered her head. Sitting back up, she reached for another tissue. "You know what's really maddening? That this happened to Chuck, of all people. I mean, he's got an arsenal over there, and he gets murdered in his own kitchen!"

Holly looked across the yard to Chuck's house. "He must have just been caught off guard."

"Chuck was never off guard." Kate's expression softened. "I remember one time after dinner, I came outside to go for a walk downtown to the supermarket. Chuck was working on his truck and had his back turned to me. I got to the driveway andI put my fanny pack around my waist. When I clicked the two ends together, he wheeled around with a pistol in his hand and I actually wet my pants."

"No way," Holly chuckled.

"Wow!" Ivy exclaimed. "Who knew the click of a fanny pack could get you killed?"

Kate laughed. "Yeah, I'd never have thought that sound could be mistaken for a gun being cocked."

Ivy wrinkled her nose. "You know, that story convinces me even more that Chuck knew whoever killed him. His guard was definitely down."

"His and the dogs'," Holly said.

"I think you're right." Kate stared across the yard. "Hey, didn't you say you had two questions?"

"Oh, yeah." Holly nodded. "When we were at Raquelle's the other night, I asked if you knew any place Tommy might hide. You started to say something, but then she came back outside and you never finished your thought."

Kate's eyes widened. "Right. You know, there was this place." Kate stood up and looked past the hen house to the field bordering the back of her property. Her eyes came to rest on the mountain in the distance. "Tommy introduced us to it. My kids and I used to hike up there with him." She seemed lost in her memory.

“Do you think he might be there?” Holly asked.

“Maybe.” Kate waggled her eyebrows. “Up for a field trip?”

18 MR. HYDE

"Good morning, Boss." Yolanda Rivera looked up from her computer screen as Nick Manelli passed her desk.

"What's so good about it?" he growled as he passed her, entered his office and slammed the door.

Officer Elva Rodriquez frowned as she stopped in front of Yolanda's desk and handed her a manila file folder. "What's up with him? He's turned from Dr. Jekyll to Mr. Hyde in just the last couple of weeks."

Yolanda leaned forward and whispered. "The Donnelly woman hasn't called here in two weeks, and that's about the time he started acting like Mr. Hyde. I think they must have split up."

"Ouch." Officer Rodriguez nodded slowly, a knowing look registering on her face. "Any idea what happened?"

"You think he's going to talk to me about it?" Yolanda sneered.

"Yeah, but weren't you friendly with Donnelly? Can't you call her?"

"Are you crazy?" Yolanda wrinkled her brow and waggled her head. "I wasn't her BFF. Besides, if Manelli found out I tried to talk to her, I'd be driving a meter maid bike again, writing parking tickets on Main Avenue."

Rodriguez chuckled. "I hear ya."

"Rivera, get in here!" a voice bellowed from behind the closed door marked *Detective Nicholas Manelli.*

"Uh-oh!" Rodriquez grinned. "Good luck," she said, heading down the corridor.

Yolanda stood, grabbing her pad and the folder Rodriguez had delivered to her. Slowly she opened the door and entered Manelli's office.

"Where's that report I asked for?" he barked, not looking up at her.

"Right here, sir," she replied, handing it to him.

Manelli took the folder, opened it and started to read.

"Sir, I did some research on that trucking company and I found out a few things."

Manelli looked up at her, narrowing his eyes. "Did I ask you to do that?"

Yolanda winced at the question. Manelli had always encouraged her initiative. She felt as if the ground had shifted under her feet. Lowering her gaze to the floor, she replied, "No, sir. Anything else, sir?"

Manelli bit his lip and looked back down at the folder in his hands. "That's all."

As the young police woman turned and headed back to the door, Manelli stood up. "Rivera?"

Yolanda turned to face him. "Yes, sir."

Walking over to his file cabinet he opened the top drawer and peered inside. “This afternoon you can show me what you found on the trucking company.”

“Okay, sir.” Rivera nodded and stepped out of the office, closing the door behind her.

She smiled, shaking her head as she heard the loud bang she knew was the sound of Manelli’s boot kicking another dent in the file cabinet.

19 FIELD TRIP

Amy led the pack up the hillside, Lucky and Winston hot on her trail.

"I swear she knows exactly where we're headed," Kate said, tugging on the strap of her backpack.

"Proves what I've always said." Holly stepped over a large rock in their path. "Dogs are way smarter than people."

Bringing up the rear, Ivy asked, "Did you come up here with her often, Kate?"

"Not often, and not in a long time," Kate replied.

"How much farther do we have to go?" Holly stopped, arms akimbo.

"If I remember correctly, we have about another half mile. Do you want to take a break?"

Simultaneously, Holly said yes and Ivy said no.

Holly stuck her tongue out at Ivy. "Oh, what the hell?" she shrugged. "Let's keep going. I'll just slow down. If I lose sight of you, I'll holler."

Fifteen minutes later, the three hikers reached their destination, but the dogs were nowhere in sight.

"There it is," said Kate.

"There what is?" Holly peered in the direction Kate pointed, unable to make out what she was pointing at.

Kate smiled. "C'mon."

"Where are the dogs?" Ivy asked.

"You'll see," was all Kate would say.

To Holly and Ivy, she appeared to be walking directly into an impenetrable wall of dark green stone. Suddenly, Lucky popped out of the wall, tail wagging wildly as she ran up to Holly.

"What in the world…" Holly continued to stare at the wall as Winston and Amy appeared.

"Up for a little spelunking?" Kate grinned, lowering her backpack and pulling a flashlight out of a zippered side pocket.

"Oh, yeah!" Ivy said following Kate to the spot where the dogs had emerged.

"A cave!" Holly remained standing motionless. "Wait a minute. You're not going in there. What if there's a -- a bear in there?

Kate made a clucking sound. "It's June. Bears are not hibernating in June."

"Besides," Ivy said, "the dogs were just in there. If there was an animal inside, they would have flushed it out."

Holly sank down on the ground. "Go spelunk all you want. I'm staying right here."

Kate shrugged. "Have it your way. C'mon Ivy."

Holly watched as the two women disappeared. Lucky came over panting and Holly poured from a water bottle into her cupped hand. As the dog lapped up the water, she asked, “You’re sure there was nothing in there. Right?” Lucky finished drinking and lay down, leaving the question unanswered.

After a few minutes, Holly looked toward the cave entrance and shouted, “Yell if you’re still alive in there.”

No reply. “Great,” Holly muttered under her breath. “No matter what, I’m not going in there, so don’t look at me that way,” she said glaring at the dog staring up at her.

At long last, Winston and Amy came out of the cave opening, followed by Kate and Ivy.

“You should go in and have a look,” Ivy said. “The rock formations are really amazing.”

“No, thanks.”

“I didn’t know you were claustrophobic.” Kate eyed Holly suspiciously.

“I’m not.” Holly shook her head. “I’m just not interested in entering dark spaces where wild animals might be lurking.”

Kate slapped her forehead. “Oh, now I remember. You’re afraid of snakes.”

Holly stood up and shivered in reply, casting a wary look around where she’d been sitting.

Ivy laughed. “That’s right. Why didn’t I think of that?”

“Never mind.” Holly frowned. “Any sign of Tommy?”

“I can’t be sure,” Kate replied, “but there is a bedroll in there.”

"Any teenager could have put it there for a rendezvous with his girlfriend," Holly scoffed.

"I know," Kate said. "But if it is Tommy, he'll know I was here looking for him. I loaded my backpack with Reese's Peanut Butter cups and Twizzlers. Those were his favorites when he was a kid. I left them with some bottles of water."

"I'm sure the local possums and whatever other varmints live around here will be very pleased when they return home."

"Stop being such a Debby Downer," Ivy scowled. "If Tommy is sleeping here, Kate left him a clear message that she'd been here to see him."

"But what good will that do?" Holly asked.

Kate slung her empty backpack over her shoulder. "I'm hoping he'll realize I'm reaching out because I want to help him and that maybe he'll get in touch with me."

Holly sighed. "That's a big maybe."

"It's all I've got." Kate shrugged. "C'mon, let's go."

"Can't we sit a little longer?" Holly asked.

"You can, but I want to go before the snake on that rock over there wakes up." Kate said as she turned back to the path leading down the mountain.

Holly pushed past her and scurried down the path, ignoring the laughter that trailed behind her.

20 BOYD REDUX

Holly stepped out onto the porch, rooting through her handbag for her car keys.

"Where are you going?" Kate asked, looking up from the herbal remedy book she was reading.

"I need to go get more dog food. I only brought enough for a few days and since we're now staying indefinitely, I need to get more. Do you need anything from the store?"

Kate sighed. "Probably, but I haven't made a list. I'll do that tomorrow."

"Okay. I'll be right back." Holly crossed the yard, got in her car and drove off.

Kate picked up her book, but before she could resume reading, Ivy stepped out onto the porch with a glass of iced tea. "What are you reading?" she asked as she dropped into a wicker chair.

"I thought I'd check up on what herbs are good for preventing infections and healing wounds."

"Good idea. I was thinking we should go over and check on Benny. I know we provided the best first aid we could, but, still, I'd like to take a look at the cut -- just to make sure he doesn't need to see a doctor."

Kate nodded. "I'm sure he doesn't have health insurance, and, even so, it's a 45 minute drive to the nearest Urgent Care facility, and then who knows how long he'd have to wait to see a doctor."

"Did you find anything helpful in your herbal book?"

Kate closed the book and sat up. "I think a poultice of St. John's Wort will do the trick. I have it growing in the side garden."

Ivy shook her head. "I've been a nurse for 30 years dealing with pharmaceutical drugs, and here you've got all these natural remedies growing in your yard."

"Well, herbs have their limits, but they certainly can't hurt."

Ivy stood up. "C'mon. Show me this St. John's Wort. I've been thinking about the perfect spot in my yard to start a healing herb garden when I get back to South Carolina."

****

Ivy surveyed the crates and piles of trash in Chuck's backyard and shook her head as Kate knocked on the back door. Razor opened the inner door and peered through the screen.

"Hi, Razor," Kate said. "We just wanted to check on the patient. How's he doing?"

"He's asleep," the big man replied, opening the door. "Come on in."

Ivy followed Kate as she stepped inside. "I hate to wake him, but I've got an herbal poultice that could help heal his wound."

"He's in here." Razor led them through the kitchen to the front sitting room where Benny lay asleep on the couch, covered in a tattered blanket.

Tapping his friend on the shoulder gently, he said, "Wake up."

Benny gave out a low moan. "Leave me alone."

Kate walked over to the couch. "Hi, Benny. Ivy and I came over to see how you're doing."

Benny blinked and raised himself on one elbow. "Oh, sorry, Kate. That's real nice of you, but I'm okay. Razor here's been checkin' on me."

"Yeah, well, Ivy wants to make sure you don't need to see a doctor, and I brought something that will help speed up the healing process and prevent infection."

"Oh, all right." Benny struggled to sit up, a sheepish grin on his face. "You two are a couple of Florence Nightindales, ain't that right, Razor?"

"Nightingales," Razor replied as he slowly removed the gauze bandage on Benny's arm.

Ivy walked over and examined the wound. Smiling, she said, "You're very lucky. There's been no more bleeding and it looks like it's already beginning to heal." She turned to Kate. "If your poultice can help speed that up, he should be fine without having to see a doctor."

Kate immediately went to work applying the poultice to Benny's wound.

"I really appreciate this," Benny said. "I hate doctors and I hate hospitals. All they do is get you addicted to them damn alkaloids."

"Opioids." Razor sighed, shaking his head.

****

Grabbing his car keys, Razor followed Kate and Ivy outside after they'd finished with Benny, who was asleep before they left.

"Going to the store. Need anything?" he asked.

"No, thanks," Kate replied. "You may run into Holly at the supermarket. She went to get dogfood."

Razor nodded. "Later," he said as he climbed in the truck and backed out of the driveway.

"A man of few words," Ivy said, smiling.

"Yeah, and he uses them all correctly."

Ivy laughed. "Do you think Benny graduated high school?"

Kate grimaced. "Sadly, yes. Does that tell you everything you need to know about our education system up here?"

As they headed back to Kate's, Lucky ran down the back steps and started to bark in the direction of the road. Amy and Winston remained on the porch.

"What's the matter, Lucky?" Ivy asked, just as the sound of a vehicle coming up the road grew louder.

Kate turned. "It's Boyd. Quick, let's get in the house before he spots us and comes begging for something."

Kate held the back door open as Ivy herded the dogs inside. "I'm going to go upstairs and get my binoculars. I want to see what he's up to."

"You really don't trust him, do you?"

"No." Kate went to her closet and retrieved the binoculars from the top shelf. As fast as she could, she pulled them out of their case and ran to the bedroom window. "He's still got Chuck's tarp on the back of his truck! I don't believe it."

"You're sure it's Chuck's tarp?" Ivy asked, arching one eyebrow.

"I'm one-hundred percent sure," Kate said, pulling a chair over to the window.

After a few minutes, Ivy said, "I'm going back downstairs to look at your herb books."

"Okay," Kate said, immobile, her eyes glued to the binoculars.

Downstairs, Ivy sank onto the living room couch and picked up Kate's copy of *Your Backyard Herb Garden*. She'd barely read a page when Lucky started growling. Winston sat up and Amy just thumped her tail. Ivy got up and went to the laundry room. Lucky followed and continued growling in front of the window that overlooked the herb bed. Ivy couldn't see anything that could be the source of Lucky's agitation. Bending down, she stroked the dog.

"It's okay, Lucky. There's no one out there." From her kneeling position, Ivy again glanced out the window.

"Uh-oh," she said under her breath as she saw Boyd stealthily moving behind the shrubs that formed the back perimeter of Kate's yard. He was headed in the direction of Chuck's back yard. The image of the thief on the tarot Seven of Wands card popped into her head. "How could I doubt you, Lucky?" She stood and ran back upstairs to Kate's bedroom.

Fixed in her surveillance position, Kate appeared not to have moved. Without taking her eyes off Boyd's truck, she asked, "What was Lucky barking at?"

"She spotted Boyd sneaking along the back over to Chuck's yard."

"What?" Kate jumped up, dropped her binoculars on the bed and ran down the stairs to the kitchen. All three dogs went to the door, wiggling anxiously.

"What are you looking for?" Ivy asked as she watched Kate search the counters.

"Something I can use as a weapon." Kate pulled open one of the drawers and pulled out a carving knife.

"Put that back right now," Ivy commanded. "For goodness sake, it's daylight. Just let the dogs loose."

"Oh, right," Kate said dropping the knife and walking to the door. As soon as she opened it, the dogs sprinted out, Lucky in the lead. By the time Ivy and Kate reached Chuck's yard, Lucky had Boyd backed up against a shed, Amy and Winston standing guard.

"Hey, call off your dog!" Boyd shouted. He tried to step forward, but Lucky snapped at his shoes, keeping him pinned in place.

Ivy ran over and grabbed the dog's collar. "It's okay, Lucky. Sit."

The dog sat, but continued to growl, not taking her eyes off Boyd.

"That dog's a menace," Boyd said, slowly stepping away from the shed.

"What are you doing back here, Boyd?" Kate asked.

"Uh, well, before Chuck -- uh, died -- he told me I could have some of his older tools." Boyd continued to edge away from Lucky and closer to Kate, a nervous smile on his face. "I just came by to pick them up."

"You need to get in touch with Flo."

Boyd's cheerless smile turned into a glare. "Look, I need those tools for a job I'm starting. I can call her later."

Unblinking, Kate crossed her arms. "Well, how about I go get my cell phone and you can talk to her right now?"

Boyd's glare intensified. "You know what you're problem is, Kate? You never could mind your own business, could you?"

As he took a step in Kate's direction, Ivy stood up gripping Lucky's collar tightly as the dog's growl grew louder. "One more step, and I'll loose this dog on you."

Boyd stood still, glancing back at Lucky. "Go ahead. I'll sue you for everything you got, and I'll make sure that mutt's put down," he snarled.

Lucky lunged, but Ivy held tight to her collar. Boyd snorted and grabbed Kate's wrist just as a truck pulled into the driveway.

"Okay, Boyd, if you don't want to talk to Flo, you can talk to him instead." Kate grinned and tilted her head in the direction of Razor as he jogged across the grass in their direction.

21 CALL HER

"Good work, Rivera," Nick said, handing her back the photos she'd printed for him. "This trucking company could be the key to solving the case. Get their phone records."

"Yes, sir," Yolanda replied, getting to her feet. She turned to the door and smiled to see Detective Archie Bendix leaning on the door jamb, a cup of coffee in both hands.

"Hello, Officer Rivera. Manelli here treating you right?" he asked. "Remember, I told you, you got a job with me anytime you want it."

Yolanda blanched. "Thanks, Detective, but like I told you before, I'm very happy here. Excuse me," she said, brushing past Bendix.

Nick glared at the rumpled detective as he walked over to his desk and handed him one of the cups of coffee. Lifting the lid and sniffing, Nick shook his head. "Hazelnut? What do you want, Archie?"

"C'mon. Can't a friend buy a friend a cup of coffee?"

"A friend, yeah. Not you."

"Nick, you keep saying things like that, and I'm gonna get offended. You know, I actually thought you were becoming civilized since you started dating Holly." Archie leaned back in his chair grinning. "How is the lovely Ms. Donnelly, by the way?"

"Why do you want to know? You need her to solve a case you're working on?"

"Oh, now, that's hitting below the belt." Archie's grin transformed to a frown. "But now that you mention it, I do have a few questions about poisonous plants."

Nick stared at Archie. "You're serious?"

"Yeah. I didn't want to call her without talking to you first. I remember how -- uh -- sensitive you were about me during the Powell investigation."

"You can call her if you want to." Nick took another sip of coffee.

Shifting in his chair, Archie stared at the detective sitting across from him. "That's it? No objections?"

Nick shrugged. "If that's all, I got to get back to work."

"Okay." Archie stood up and paused when he got to the door. "Wait a minute." Closing the door he sat back down, a real look of concern on his face. "You and her didn't split up, did you?"

Not looking up, Nick said, "I'm busy, Archie. Good-bye."

The older detective placed his elbow on the desk edge and rested his chin in his hand. "Nick, what the hell happened? I know you were crazy about her."

Nick turned a page, his eyes focused on the report in front of him.

Archie heaved a sigh of exasperation. "You and I go back a long way. I know it ain't been easy for you since Anna Marie died."

After a few moments of silence, Nick glanced up. "Oh, you still here?"

Archie shook his head. "Okay," he said, standing up. "I'm going, but I gotta say one thing. All kidding aside. You know, I think of you as a son. Whatever you did, pick up the phone, call her and tell her you're sorry."

Out in the hall, Yolanda watched Archie head to the exit and grimaced as she heard the file cabinet take another blow.

22 A PHONE CALL

"You should have seen Boyd's face!" Kate giggled.

"Yeah, you really missed it, Holly." Ivy chortled. "He even volunteered to return the tarp before Razor ever said a word."

Kate gave out a belly laugh. "And after he gave it back, all Razor said was, 'I'll tell Flo you returned this.' Boyd actually stuttered. 'N-n-not necessary' and ran down the driveway."

"Quite a guy, this Boyd. Sorry, I'm never here when he shows up. Could you pass me the salad?" Holly asked.

Kate handed the salad bowl across the table. "I don't know who he's more afraid of -- Lucky, Razor or Flo."

"Remember how you felt the day Benny and Razor arrived?" Ivy asked.

"Yeah, yeah. I don't need another I-told-you-so." Kate nodded. "I now hope these guys never leave. They make far better neighbors than Flo."

"Where is Flo, by the way?" Holly asked.

"Good question," Kate replied. "She seemed all hot and ready to clear out the place yesterday."

"I looked around the property when we went over there this morning." Ivy's eyes widened. "It's going to take weeks to get rid of everything."

Kate stood up and started to collect the empty plates and silverware. "Yeah, Chuck was a bit of a hoarder. I'm just glad it's not my problem. Dessert anyone?"

Ivy grinned. "Let me help you."

Kate cut the apple pie and just as Ivy started to load the dishwasher, the phone rang.

"I don't recognize this number," Kate said, looking at the caller ID.

"Probably a sales call." Ivy picked up two dessert plates and headed back to the dining room. "This looks so delicious." Ivy handed Holly a plate, then sat down admiring the slice of pie in front of her.

"I swear, you enjoy looking at food almost as much as eating it." Holly shook her head.

"Don't listen to her," Kate said, returning to her chair. "As my grandmother would say, 'Mangia e divertiti'."

Ivy smiled as she lifted a piece of the pie to her mouth. "Yum -- as good as it looks!"

Before Kate could take a bite, the phone rang again. A puzzled look crossed her face. "Excuse me," she said and went back to the kitchen, lifted the handset and looked at the caller ID screen. The same number as before. This time she answered.

"Hello."

"Kate, it's me -- Tommy. Got your candygram."

"Tommy, are you okay?"

"Yeah, I'm fine."

"Where you calling from?"

Tommy laughed. “You know how hard it is to find a working payphone these days? I just want you to tell my mother I’m okay and not to worry.”

“You’re kidding, right? She’s beside herself. You need to come home.”

“Can’t do that right now.”

“I’ll help you. I know you didn’t kill Chuck.”

“Thanks for the vote of confidence, but there’s more than that going on. Just tell my mother I’m okay.”

“Tommy…” Kate stopped when she heard the dial tone. Putting the phone down, she turned around. Holly and Ivy stood in the dining room doorway.

“Well?” Holly said.

“He’s alright, but he said he can’t come home. That there’s more than Chuck’s murder going on.”

“What do you think that means?” Ivy asked.

Holly shook her head slowly. “I really don’t think I want to know the answer to that question.”

23 SLEEPLESS IN REDDINGTON MANOR

Holly stared at herself in the bathroom mirror as she rinsed her toothbrush. Tommy's phone call left her feeling unsettled. What had he meant when he said there was more than Chuck's murder going on? As if that wasn't enough to worry about.

Feeling exhausted, she returned to her bedroom. Maybe she'd get a good night's sleep. She pulled down the covers and started to get into bed when she remembered she needed to charge her cell phone. Going over to the dresser, she picked up the phone and the charger.

She hadn't checked her e-mail since the morning, so she turned on the phone and punched in her security code. A small red number "1" appeared on the phone icon. Another unknown number to block. Tapping on the green box, she froze when she saw Nick's name and number.

Her skin tingled as she sank down on the bed. She drew in a deep breath, her finger poised above the delete button. Shaking her head, she tapped the "Play" button instead.

"Holly, it's me. Call me."

A tear rolled down her cheek. She covered her mouth to stifle a sob. The last thing she wanted was her sister or Kate to hear her. Dropping down on the bed, she cried into her pillow.

After a few minutes she sat back up and replayed the short message. Should she call? Her finger hovered over the Call Back icon. No. What was the point? Grabbing her Kindle, she propped up her pillows and started to read. After a paragraph, she stopped, unable to remember one word of what she'd just read. She didn't need to hit replay. Nick's message echoed in her head. How was she ever going to fall asleep?

After another half hour of tossing and turning, Holly got out of bed and reached for her robe. Carefully opening her bedroom door, she tried not to make a sound. Out in the hall, she was relieved to see no lights under Ivy's and Kate's doors. Slowly, she tiptoed downstairs. When she turned on the light in the living room, Amy and Winston just looked up without lifting their heads. Lucky got up and came to her, tail wagging.

Holly gave her a pat on the head, grabbed the remote and settled down on the recliner. After channel surfing for a few minutes, she selected a re-run of *The Nanny*. Whenever she had problems falling asleep, watching television helped. If the show didn't put her out, the first string of commercials almost always lulled her into a mindless state and she'd be asleep before the show resumed. Tonight took two sets of commercials, but finally she drifted off somewhere in the middle of a used-car salesman's pitch.

A few hours later, Lucky's cold nose nudged Holly's arm. "Go away," she said, but the dog butted her hand again. Holly blinked and glared at her. "Just when I finally fell asleep." Lucky continued to stare at

Holly, tail moving like a metronome. That could only mean one thing. Sighing, she sat up and put on her slippers. “Let’s go.”

The microwave clock in the kitchen read 3:23 AM. Grabbing a flashlight from the kitchen counter, Holly unlocked the back door. Turning, she shook her head. Amy and Winston had followed them to the kitchen.

“No way,” she said. “I don’t trust you two off the leash, and I certainly don’t feel like having my arms pulled out of their sockets.” She grabbed Lucky’s leash, though she didn’t think she’d need it. Guiding Amy and Winston away from the door, she let Lucky out, then backed out herself. Lucky ran down the steps and out onto the grass.

The full moon lit the yard and Holly could see all the way back to the recently installed chicken coop. She descended the porch steps and waited, grateful no deer or other more worrisome critters were about. Lucky moved down the yard sniffing. The dog squatted and Holly smiled. “That was quick,” she said into the night air.

Lucky turned and headed back, but midway down the long expanse of yard she veered off around the back of the house. Holly rolled her eyes and sighed. She didn’t want to disturb the peace by yelling for the dog, so she decided to just wait for her to return.

After a few minutes Holly remembered the deep ravine that separated Kate’s house from the Leggett house. She hoped Lucky hadn’t gone down there and decided she better go find here. No telling what she’d bring back from down there.

Moving the flashlight beam back and forth in a wide arc, Holly crossed the yard. She could feel the wetness of the grass penetrating her slippers.

Turning the corner of the house, she was relieved to see the dog by the side porch.

"Lucky, c'mon," she said in a stage whisper.

The dog didn't respond. Instead, she lowered herself onto her front paws. Her butt up in the air wiggled as she stuck her nose under the porch.

"Oh, no!" Holly ran over when she remembered Kate said a groundhog sometimes took up residence under there. "Lucky, no!" She reached for the dog's collar, attached the leash and tugged. "Come out of there."

On the last tug, Holly lost her grip and fell backwards landing flat on her back. "Great. Just great," she said aloud as she struggled her way up to a sitting position, facing the Leggett house. That's when she noticed a light in the window that faced her bedroom. Still holding onto the flashlight, she aimed the beam at the window. Holly gasped as a man's ghoulish face appeared. He spotted her, then quickly disappeared. The light went out.

Holly scrambled to her feet, caught hold of Lucky's leash and pulled.

"Let's go!" she commanded and this time the dog followed. Together they ran around the back of the house. Her heart was racing as they bounded up the porch steps.

Inside, Holly slid the barrel bolt lock, turned the deadbolt and shut off the lights. Scurrying into the living room, she found the remote and shut off the television. She mounted the stairs as quickly as she could and went straight to her bedroom window, peering out across the ravine. She stood watching, trying to catch her breath. No lights. No movement. No sounds. Climbing into bed, she pulled the covers over her head. What fresh hell is this?

24 ALTERNATE PLAN B

Ivy and Kate stared at Holly as she stepped out onto the porch with her mug of coffee.

"What's wrong with you?" Ivy asked, closing the herbal book in her lap.

"Why would you ask me that?"

Kate put down the newspaper she was reading. "Even I have to say you look terrible. Didn't you sleep well again?"

Holly slumped down onto a wicker chair. "No, I did not. I hardly slept at all."

Kate chuckled. "I'd have thought after our hike yesterday, you would have slept like a baby."

"Maybe you need to make a doctor's appointment when we get back to New Jersey," Ivy said, a look of concern on her face.

"I don't need a doctor. I just need a good night's sleep." Holly bit her lower lip. "I saw something next door last night."

"What?" Kate asked.

"A face. A man's face. In the upstairs window."

Ivy moved to the edge of her chair. "What are you talking about?"

Holly recounted her actions of the night before.

"Are you crazy?" Ivy shook her head. "You should never have gone outside alone at 3:30 in the morning. There's a killer on the loose here."

Kate stood up and placed her arms on her hips. "Besides, how many times have I told you not to let the dog off the leash after dark? There are wild animals that come into the yard. What would you have done if Lucky ran out of the yard after a deer? Go after her in your pajamas?"

"That's rich coming from the woman who went out in the dark two nights ago armed with a broom," Holly sneered.

"Did you even have a broom?" Kate glared at her. "You never…"

"It must have been Boyd," Ivy interjected.

Kate's shoulders sagged and she sat back down. "You're right."

"Whoever it was looked like a ghoul." Holly took another sip of coffee.

"Yeah, that's Boyd." Kate nodded.

Ivy's expression turned glum. "If it was him, that's his mother's house. He has every right to be there."

"Then why did he put the light out when he saw Holly? And what's he doing there in the middle of the night anyway?" Kate asked.

"He was probably afraid to come back during the day after you all confronted him yesterday." Holly answered.

“Still -- I don’t like it,” Kate said. “Was his truck in the driveway?”

“I don’t know. I don’t remember seeing anything, but I wasn’t looking for it. Like I said, after I saw the face and he saw me, I grabbed the dog and ran. When I got back upstairs, I looked out my window, but I saw no movement and never heard anything either.”

“Well, you certainly would have heard a truck.” Kate got up and walked across the porch to the other side of the house. When she was out of view, Ivy looked at Holly.

“I don’t like this either. This is getting scary.”

“I agree. I just want to go home.” Holly sighed.

“We can’t leave Kate alone here. Do you think we could talk her into coming with us? At least until they catch the killer.”

Holly smiled. “That’s exactly what I was thinking yesterday.”

Before she could say more, Kate returned. “You can’t really see anything from the porch.” She dropped down on a chair and almost immediately sprang back up. “I know. Let’s go over around the back way -- the way Boyd crossed over to Chuck’s yesterday -- and see if we can get inside. Maybe we could find a clue.”

Ivy’s eyes widened and Holly jumped to her feet. “You, my friend, are out of control. Ivy and I discussed it -- we’re packing up and going to my place and you’re coming with us.”

“No, I’m not.” Kate replied, a steely look in her eyes.

“Oh, yes you are!” Holly’s head bobbed like a dashboard doll’s.

"Okay, stop." Ivy stepped in between the two, placing a hand on Kate's arm. "I agree with Holly. We've been involved in murder investigations before and we both nearly got killed."

"I get that," Kate replied, her attitude ratcheted down a notch from her reaction to Holly's suggestion. "But..."

"No, but's," Holly said. "I hate to bring him up, but I remember what Nick said to me. 'Murder isn't a parlor game.' Suggesting we break the law by trespassing takes this way beyond the parlor game stage."

"Oh, like you haven't done the same thing..."

"Stop!" Ivy held up her hands, a palm in each of their faces. "What you just suggested is dangerous, Kate. For all you know, Boyd could have stolen property over there, or even dead bodies. What would you do then? Call Cyrus Bascom? And say what?"

Kate hesitated, then dropped into her chair, covering her face with her hands. "Oh, brother. You're right."

Holly mouthed the words "thank you" to Ivy, walked over to Kate and squeezed her shoulder. "It's just for a few days."

"Okay. Maybe that would be best. Ugh!" She leaned back in the chair. "What about the dogs -- and the chickens?"

"You can bring the dogs," Holly reassured her. "We'll just have to take two cars."

"I'll drive with you, Kate," Ivy offered. "And I'm sure Benny and Razor will take care of the chickens."

Kate sighed. "All right. I'll start packing."

Ivy looked at her watch. “It’s already after ten. What do you say we leave after lunch?”

Kate frowned. “I was going to go to the supermarket this morning. I don’t have any food to make lunch.”

“No, problem,” Holly said. “Let’s pack, then go downtown and eat at the sandwich shop. We can come back and get the dogs after we eat.”

“Sounds like a plan,” Kate said as all three women stood up and went inside.

****

“Isn’t that Flo?” Holly asked.

Kate finished locking the door and looked across the yard to the driveway as Flo’s gray Kia came to a stop. “Yep. Good. I want to talk to her.”

When they reached the car, Flo was already talking to Ivy who’d been waiting beside Holly’s car. “I was just telling your friend here that I appreciate what she did for Benny. He told me what happened here yesterday. Thanks for keeping an eye on the place, Kate.”

“No problem.” Kate smiled. “Listen, Flo, after lunch we’re leaving for New Jersey. I’m going to stay with Holly and Ivy for a few days.”

“You want Benny to keep an eye on your place?”

“Yeah. That would be great. I just want you to know that Boyd was in the Leggett house in the middle of the night last night.”

“Oh, that does it! I’m calling Cyrus. And if he doesn’t take care of that low-life, I will.”

25 MAIN STREET DELI

"I don't know why I didn't think of calling Flo about Boyd," Kate shook her head. "I feel much better now."

"Good," Holly laughed as she pulled into a parking spot in front of the Main Street Deli. "I was worried we were going to have to hog tie you in order to get you to leave with us this afternoon."

"Oh, my goodness!" Kate exclaimed as she got out of the car. "There's Raquelle going into the gift shop. I forgot all about calling her. Let me run over there."

"Wait," Ivy said. "I'll go with you. Holly, would you mind ordering the sandwiches while we go over there?"

"Hungry or not, you can't pass up a chance to go into a gift shop, can you?" Holly chuckled.

After a brief discussion of what to order, Kate and Ivy crossed the street and headed down the block.

As Holly was about to open the deli door, someone tapped her on the shoulder. Turning around, she faced a chunky brunette who smiled at her. Holly guessed she was in her 30’s. Wearing blue jeans and an oversized tee-shirt, the woman pointed to the alley where some picnic tables stood.

“You want to come this way,” she said. “They’re taking orders through the back pick-up window.”

Holly hesitated.

“C’mon.” The brunette nodded encouragingly. “You’ll get your order faster.”

“Okay,” Holly said.

The woman stepped aside and extended her arm the way a maître’d would. Holly thanked her and started down the alley. As she reached the end of the red brick building, she got an uneasy feeling. It seemed too quiet. She turned back to check with the woman, but she was nowhere in sight. That was the last thing Holly remembered.

26 SURPRISE

By the time Kate and Ivy reached the gift shop, Raquelle was on her way out.

"Hi, Raquelle. I need to talk to you," Kate said, taking her by the arm.

"I'll just be inside." Ivy smiled and entered the store.

"What is it?" Raquelle asked.

Kate looked over her shoulder, then leaned in close and whispered. "I got a call from Tommy."

"What! Where is he?"

"Ssh!" Kate pulled the tall blonde farther away from the shop door. "He wouldn't tell me where he is. He just told me to tell you he's all right."

Raquelle pulled her arm away. "Why'd he call you and not me?"

"I sort of left him a message."

Eyes blazing, Raquelle asked. "How did you get a message to him if you don't know where he is?"

Kate grimaced. "I left some Twizzlers and Reese's Peanut Butter Cups up in a cave we used to go to with my kids. I just took a chance he might go there, and I wanted him to know I was thinking of him."

"I want you to take me to that cave," Raquelle demanded.

"He won't go back there now. You know that."

The distraught mother looked away. Kate put her hand on Raquelle's shoulder. "He knows the woods better than anyone. He'll be okay."

Raquelle wiped away a tear in the corner of her eye. "I hope you're right." Without looking back, she crossed the street and got into her car.

Kate watched as she drove off. Turning she entered the gift shop and found Ivy sifting through a box of costume jewelry.

"How'd it go?" she asked.

"About as well as can be expected," Kate replied. "I feel so bad for her. If it were my son, I'd be insane right about now."

Ivy nodded. "At least she knows he's okay."

"As of last night, anyway."

Ivy settled on a blue butterfly pin. After paying at the checkout register, she and Kate made their way to the sandwich shop.

"Where's Holly?" Ivy looked around the small deli, putting her bag down on a table near the front door.

Kate shrugged and walked up to the counter. "Hi. Is someone in your restroom?"

"No." The apron-clad woman shook her head. "Can I take your order?"

Kate looked puzzled. "Didn't a woman come in about ten minutes ago and place an order for three sandwiches?"

"No. Nobody's been in here in the last half hour."

Kate walked back to the table where Ivy was sitting. "She's not here."

"What do you mean?" Ivy asked, looking confused.

"The woman said she never came in."

Ivy's face drained of color. "How can that be?" She jumped up and went to the door. "Maybe she's outside."

In front of the deli, they peered up and down the street. Ivy tried the car door.

"Still locked," she said. "I'm getting a very bad feeling about this."

"Hold on," Kate said calmly. "Maybe she went to the supermarket to get some drinks for the drive this afternoon. Let's go check there."

Ivy nodded and ran across the street. Kate had to run to catch up with her. Inside the supermarket, Ivy raced across the store looking down each aisle. Kate approached a teen-aged boy working checkout and asked if he'd seen Holly.

"She's about 5'3", blonde hair in a ponytail -- wearing black shorts and a pink tee-shirt."

"Nope," said the heavily tattooed young man. I've been on this register for an hour. Haven't seen anyone who looks like that."

Ivy met Kate at the register, shaking her head. "She's not in here."

Kate pointed at the cashier. "He says he hasn't seen her either."

Kate followed Ivy back out to the parking lot. "What do you say we split up? Let's go in each of the stores? There's only ten. She's got to be in one of them."

Ivy nodded and headed to the realtor's. Kate crossed the street and started with the bookstore.

Fifteen minutes later, Ivy ran to the car where Kate waited. "Any luck?" she asked.

Kate shook her head.

Ivy's shoulders sagged. "This can't be happening. How can no one have seen her?"

"I don't know," Kate replied, gazing in through the deli window one last time. "Wait a minute." She turned to the alleyway and ran past the picnic tables to the back of the building, out of sight. Ivy followed, but before she reached the back, Kate reappeared, her face expressionless, Holly's shoulder bag in her hand.

27 MISSING PERSON

Ivy leaned against the car, clutching Holly's bag to her chest. Kate paced back and forth in front of the deli. She stopped as the police cruiser came into sight and pulled into the parking spot behind Holly's Cadillac CTS.

Sheriff Bascom got out of the police car and approached the women, a stern expression on his face. Deputy Bascom followed and stood off to the side.

"Okay, ladies. What's this about your friend disappearing?" he asked, his tone harsh.

"My *sister*, Sheriff." Ivy corrected, her tone icy.

Appearing chagrined, Bascom took off his hat. "Sorry, Ms. Donnelly. Why don't you tell me what happened."

Ivy recounted their every move since Holly'd parked the car. "Kate found Holly's handbag behind the deli. Her car keys are in here, but her wallet's gone. That's when we called you."

The sheriff tipped his head in the direction of the alley. The deputy nodded and made his way past the picnic tables to the back of the building.

Bascom hesitated. “Now, I don’t mean to offend you -- but I know sisters can sometimes tease one another. Could your sister just be playing a trick on you--some kind a practical joke?”

“Sheriff Bascom!” Kate exclaimed, outrage pouring out of her.

“Kate,” Ivy said, grabbing her by the arm. Her calm, commanding tone stopped Kate before she could say anymore. Ivy’s eyes met Bascom’s, and held them for a moment before she replied. “No, Sheriff. Holly is not a practical joker. We came downtown to get lunch. We’re -- we were planning to return to New Jersey this afternoon. Kate, too. Holly was anxious to get on the road so we could avoid arriving during rush hour.”

The sheriff blinked and looked down at the hat in his hands.

“This has to have something to do with what happened last night,” Kate interjected.

“What happened last night?” Bascom asked, his expression shifting from concerned to annoyed.

“When Holly took the dog out in the middle of the night, she saw a man in the upstairs window of the Leggett house,” Kate replied. “I’m sure it was Boyd. By the way, didn’t Flo call you about him trying to steal tools the other day?”

Bascom glared at her. “First of all, who calls me is none of your business, Ms. Farmer. Secondly, how could Ms. Donnelly see into that house in the middle of the night? There’s no electricity.”

Before Kate could react, Ivy said, “Holly had a flashlight. Maybe whoever was in the house did, too. She said she slipped in the grass and when she looked up there was a light in the window. A man was looking down at her.”

Bascom bit his lower lip, looking from Ivy to the hat he slowly rotated in his hand. "A man, you say. Did she identify him as Boyd Leggett?"

Ivy shook her head. "She's never seen Boyd."

"Who else could it be?" Kate asked, her fists clenched.

Bascom's mouth turned up in a sour smile. "We've had our share of squatters and break-ins in this town. You know that. Could be some drifter just discovered that abandoned place and decided to stay the night."

"Oh, c'mon..." Kate leaned towards the sheriff. "It could also be whoever killed Chuck."

Ivy stepped in between Kate and Bascom.

"Sheriff," she said. "I don't know who was in that house or if it had anything to do with this. All I know is my sister is missing." She held up Holly's shoulder bag. "This is proof she didn't just go off and leave us here. Please..." Her voice broke and she lowered her head.

Bascom just watched as Kate put her arm around Ivy. Turning to the alley, he appeared relieved to see his deputy returning.

"I followed some tire tracks back to the next street and found this. It's empty." Jason Bascom held up a wallet.

Ivy walked over to him. Tears filled her eyes as she nodded. "It's Holly's."

28 WHAT TO DO?

Ivy brought the Cadillac to a stop in front of Kate's garage. They had driven back from downtown in silence. When they got out of the car, they both looked up at the second floor window where all three of the dogs barked down to them in greeting.

"I'm glad someone's happy," Kate said.

When she opened the kitchen door, the three dogs flew out, jumping jubilantly around the two women. Lucky sniffed each of them briefly, then ran past them down the steps to the car.

As the dog sniffed the car door, looking up at the driver-side window for her mistress, Ivy sank down on the steps and began sobbing. Kate lowered her head, fighting back her own tears.

"Hey, Kate," Benny called from the driveway next door. Frowning, she gave him a weak wave. He looked from her to Ivy and headed towards them. His cheerful smile turned into a look of concern the closer he got. "Hey, what's the matter, Ivy?" When she didn't look up, he turned his gaze to Kate.

"Somebody's kidnapped Holly," Kate said in response to his quizzical expression.

"No," he said in disbelief. Sinking down on the step beside Ivy, he put his arm around her and gently rested his head on hers.

When Razor came out of the house next door, he looked over and immediately started across the grass. "What happened?" He clenched and unclenched his fists, his whole body bristling. "Did someone hurt you?"

"Her sister got kidnapped," Benny said.

"Boyd," was all the big man said.

Kate dropped onto a wicker chair, a grim smile on her face. "That's what I said. Did Flo tell you we think Holly saw him in the house last night?"

"Yeah," Benny said. "She called the sheriff again, but she didn't get to talk to him. She gave his secretary hell. Wait till she hears this."

Kate huffed. "Yeah, well, tell her that even after Jason found Holly's wallet in the road, we still had to argue with Bascom for about ten minutes before he finally agreed to go over to Boyd's girlfriend's to question him."

Razor shook his head. Kneeling on one knee in front of Ivy, he took both her hands in his. "Don't worry, little sister. We'll find her."

Ivy lifted her head and just nodded.

Razor stood back up and headed to the truck. "C'mon, Benny."

"Where we going?"

When Razor didn't reply, Benny took his arm from around Ivy and got up. "I better go." He squeezed Ivy's hand, nodded to Kate and ran after his friend.

"Do you think they can find her?" Ivy asked as she watched them drive off.

Kate sighed. "I don't know. I just hope they don't do anything that lands them in jail." Standing up, she said, "Let's go in and try to find something to eat."

Ivy shook her head. "I'm not hungry."

"Not something I ever thought I'd hear you say, but c'mon. You have to eat."

****

After a lunch of canned chicken soup, Kate and Ivy took the dogs for a walk. Ivy went reluctantly. She didn't want to leave the phone, hopeful the sheriff would call. As they made their way up the road towards Raquelle's house, she remembered when she'd been abducted after Mrs. Hagel's murder.

Suddenly, she said, "We have to do something. When it was me who was kidnapped, Holly did everything she could to rescue me."

Kate frowned. "I know. But I've been racking my brain and I can't think of anything we can do. Not yet anyway. Your kidnapper called Holly and told her what he wanted. We don't know what Boyd -- or whoever took her -- wants."

Ivy groaned. "That's just it. What if he doesn't want anything? What if he just wants to shut her up? She could be dead already!"

"Don't say that," Kate commanded. She tugged on the dogs' leashes and turned back homeward. "I know what we'll do. C'mon."

29 KING OF WANDS

Kate knelt on the floor in front of the coffee table. Ivy sat on the couch and watched as she shuffled the Tarot deck.

"Do you really think this will help?" she asked shaking her head.

"Are you seriously asking me that question?" Kate glared at her.

"Sorry. But you're not going to ask if she's dead, are you?" Ivy cast a tortured look at Kate.

"No," Kate said. "I'm just going to do a three-card spread. What we want is any advice the cards can give us about how we can help Holly."

Ivy nodded and took a deep breath as Kate peeled off the first card.

"Oh, no," gasped Ivy.

The Eight of Swords showed a woman blindfolded, bound by ropes and surrounded by swords.

"Just hold on," Kate said. "I admit this looks bad, but I'm taking it to mean she's a captive, but she's alive." Continuing, she turned over the second card. "The Hanged Man."

Ivy groaned.

Kate shook her head. "Again, don't panic. Actually, one meaning of this card is about waiting and having patience -- literally it's about just hanging in there. If the first card is Holly, I think this one is for us." Finally she turned over the third card and smiled. "The King of Wands."

"Nick!" Ivy said. "That's it. We have to call him. He'll know what to do." She jumped up and ran to the stairs.

"Where are you going?"

"Upstairs. I think I have his card in my wallet."

"Wait a minute," Kate said. "Remember the cards seem to be cautioning us to wait."

"You can wait. I'm calling Nick." Ivy mounted the remaining stairs two at a time.

Kate had just put the Tarot cards back in their box, when Ivy flew down the steps.

"Look what I found when I went in Holly's room." She held out Holly's cellphone.

Kate grabbed the phone and turned it on. Peering at the screen she said, "I don't believe it!"

"What?" Ivy leaned over to look at the screen.

"There's a message from Nick." Kate hit the play button.

"Holly, it's me. Call me."

"Give me that." Ivy grabbed the phone, hit the call back button and put it on speakerphone.

Nick answered after just two rings. "Holly."

"No, Nick. It's Ivy."

"Ivy!" Nick laughed warmly. "You know, Holly hasn't been returning my calls. I was just thinking about calling you."

"Nick, I'm up at Kate's in Reddington Manor. There's been a murder and Holly's been kidnapped."

"Text me the address. I'll call you from the car. I'm on my way."

30 A DAY TOO LONG

Holly opened her eyes. Her head ached, and when she tried to sit up, she realized her right arm was handcuffed to the bedpost. She looked up at the ceiling. Brown water spots ringed the corners and faded wall paper curled at the seams. The room had a musty smell.

Wincing, she tried to sit up. Lifting her head was an effort. She sidled back against the headboard, finally managing to get into a sitting position. A yellowed window shade covered the only window on the wall opposite the bed. The silhouette of tree branches swaying in the breeze was visible through the shade. She must be in an upstairs bedroom.

Holly looked down at the bed and saw there were no sheets and a coil spring was visible through a hole in the mattress. *Oh, God, please don't let there be bedbugs or lice.*

Where was she? How did she get here? She struggled to remember. Weren't they going to drive to New Jersey this afternoon? Her stomach gurgled and she realized she was hungry. *That's it.* She was supposed to order sandwiches. Finally, it all came back to her. She recalled the woman who told her to go to the back of the deli to place her order.

"Self-defense Lesson Number One. When alone, always be aware of your surroundings."

Holly shook her head and sighed as she remembered the night Nick said those words to her at the airport. She was making room for his suitcase in the trunk of her car when he sneaked up behind her, covered her mouth and put her in the trunk. She'd been so angry at him. But he was right. He was always right, damn him! She'd bet he'd be laughing at her right now.

Or would he? Probably not. She'd give anything to see his smiling, bossy face right now. He'd rescued her more than once. But there was no chance he was coming to save her this time. He couldn't know where she was. *She* didn't know where she was.

Her arm ached. She stood up, but couldn't even take a step. Changing her position did ease the pain in her wrist. When a bird tweeted outside, she realized it was the first sound she'd heard since she came to. She focused on listening for any type of noise that could help her identify where she might be. Nothing -- not even the hum of traffic in the distance. She had to be in the middle of nowhere.

Suddenly, she thought of Ivy and Kate. They must be frantic. Had they gotten back to the deli in time to see anything? She sat back down and sighed. Ivy had gone with Kate because of the gift shop. She could linger over trinkets and souvenirs for hours. Highly unlikely they returned to the deli by the time she was rendered unconscious.

The words of a Bob Dylan song popped into her head. "The only thing I did wrong, I stayed in Mississippi a day too long." She snorted thinking the only thing she did wrong was stay in Reddington Manor an hour too long. If only they'd packed up the car and gotten lunch on the road, she wouldn't be here. Why did they go downtown? Why did they split up? She filled her cheeks with air and slowly exhaled.

Wait a minute. Why am I even here?

A memory of the ghoulish face she'd seen in the window next door pushed Bob Dylan's tune right out of her mind. But why would someone abduct her just because she'd seen a face in a window. Whatever was going on next door had to be illegal. Maybe like Ivy suggested, Boyd was storing stolen property there -- or drugs -- or dead bodies…

The sound of an engine made Holly sit up. Her heartbeat picked up speed as the sound grew closer and came to a stop nearby. She heard voices, but couldn't make out what they were saying. She looked around to see if there was anything she could use to defend herself. Nothing. She lay back down and pretended to be asleep as she heard footsteps mounting the stairs.

31 PESTO

Nick pulled into Kate's driveway a little past ten o'clock. Ivy rushed outside and ran to the car, but Lucky got there first. The dog jumped up and down, yipping manically. Nick knelt down in an effort to calm her.

"Yeah, I missed you, too," he said rubbing behind Lucky's ears. Standing up, he hugged Ivy in a tight embrace.

"Oh, Nick. I'm so glad you're here. C'mon inside."

"Kate," he said when they entered the kitchen.

"Hey, Nick." She waved from in front of the stove. "Hungry? I made pesto. Ivy hardly ate anything, so there's plenty."

"Sure," he said, dropping his keys on the kitchen island counter.

Ivy pulled out a chair for him. "We called the sheriff after our conversation with you in the car. He said no one was at Boyd's girlfriend's house. None of the neighbors saw either him or her since the day before yesterday."

Kate loaded pasta onto a plate and handed it to Nick. "I asked the sheriff to have someone stake out the place but he wouldn't," she said as she got him silverware and a napkin. "Glass of wine?"

"Just water, thanks," he said as he sat down.

Ivy got a glass out of the cupboard. "He did say he told the neighbors to call 911 if they saw anyone come in or out of the place."

"What about the guys next door?" Nick asked.

"They haven't come back since they left this afternoon," Ivy replied.

"To be honest, I'm a little worried about them," Kate added.

"Based on your description, I think they know how to take care of themselves -- at least the sharp one." Nick twirled his fork in the pasta.

Kate laughed. "You mean Razor?"

Nick nodded as he tasted his first forkful. "Good pesto."

"Well, what do you think?" Ivy asked, sinking into the chair beside him. "Do you think she's …"

"I think we need to get inside the house next door."

"That's exactly what I said." Kate smiled and poured herself some wine. "Finally someone with some sense."

"You're not actually going to break in there, are you?" Ivy asked, her eyes opened wide.

Nick smiled. "No. First thing tomorrow, I'll go down to talk to the sheriff and -- uh -- suggest he get a warrant."

"Really?" Kate looked disappointed. "I think we should go in the back way right now." A cellphone chirp interrupted her. She looked down at her phone resting on the counter. “Oh, excuse me. That’s my daughter.” Picking up the phone she walked into the living room.

“I didn’t realize she was a little crazy,” Nick said.

Ivy sighed. “Not as crazy as I feel. Oh, Nick, I’m so worried. This isn’t a kidnapping. Whoever took Holly doesn’t want anything from us. They just took her…” She covered her face with her hands.

Nick lay down his fork, put a hand on her shoulder and squeezed. “I’ll find her.”

Ivy dropped her hands and stared at him through tear filled eyes. “You still love her.”

“Of course,” he said.

“Then why did you break up with her?”

This time Nick sighed. “Is that what she told you?”

Ivy furrowed her brow. “All she would say was that you broke up and she wouldn’t talk about it.”

“She broke it off.”

“What!” Ivy exclaimed. She jumped up and walked across the kitchen, looked out the window into the dark, then turned back to face him. “You better find her, and when you do, *I’m* going to kill her.”

Nick smiled, picked up his fork and resumed twirling pasta onto his fork. Kate reappeared in the doorway. “Kill who?”

“My sister,” Ivy said, crossing her arms, leaning against the counter.

“Wait -- what?” Kate said, appearing bewildered.

“*Holly* broke up with Nick.” Ivy waggled her head.

Kate nodded. “I should have known. More pasta, *Paisan?*”

Nick shook his head. “I’m good.”

“Why did she break up with you?” Ivy asked.

“Oh, let me answer that.” Kate held up her hands, palms outward. “She panicked.” Looking at Nick she asked, “What? Did you ask her to set a wedding date?”

Nick leaned back in his chair. “Bingo.”

Ivy clenched her fists. “I don’t believe this! Why didn’t you call me?”

“I was planning to,” Nick replied. “I thought I’d give her some time first.”

“Great,” Ivy grumbled. “Just great. When I see her…” Ivy’s shoulders sagged and she lowered her head.

Nick got up, walked over and put an arm around her. “When I find her, I’m counting on you to talk some sense into her.” She looked up, giving him a weak smile.

“Do you really think she’s still…”

“I wouldn’t be here if I didn’t.”

32 HELP!

Holly remained still, her eyes closed as the door opened.

"Wake up," a woman's voice commanded.

Holly blinked her eyes open. In front of her stood a woman in a rubber Halloween witch's mask that covered her entire head and neck. She aimed a small pistol at her.

"I'm gonna take you to the bathroom." She reached over and unlocked the handcuffs.

"Why am I here?" Holly asked as she sat up and rubbed her wrist.

"Just get up."

Holly wobbled when she stood, a bit unsteady on her feet. The witch grabbed her by the elbow and pulled her forward through the doorway into a narrow hall. All Holly managed to see were two closed doors and another window with the shade pulled down.

"Hurry it up in there," the witch said.

Holly didn't need any prompting. She had no idea how much time had passed since she last used a rest room. She desperately needed to relieve herself and wasted no time once the woman pushed her inside the small bathroom.

To her left, a small sink sat next to the toilet, cracked and stained. Barely an inch separated the sink and a white, claw foot tub that extended from wall to wall. Holly shook her head thinking of how much the tub would go for at an antique store.

Over her shoulder, she noticed a small window above the tub, but frowned when she saw it was painted black. Too small for her to fit through anyway.

"You done in there?" The witch pounded on the door.

"Almost," Holly replied as she stood up and zipped her shorts. Only a trickle came through the spigot when she turned on the water. No soap. A distorted image looked back at her from the broken mirror of the medicine cabinet. She snorted thinking of Picasso's *Woman with Artichoke.*

Shutting off the water she looked around, but there was nothing to dry her hands with. Instead she shook them and slid them down the back of her shorts. She was about to open the medicine cabinet when the door hit her in the back.

Holly turned and glared at her captor. "That's a good look for you."

"Shut up." The woman grabbed her wrist and twisted her arm. Holly winced as she was dragged across the hall back to the bedroom. The woman pushed her down and put the handcuff back on her wrist. She went back out in the hall and returned with a paper bag she thrust at Holly.

Holly held on to the bag with her free hand. "Why am I here?" she asked once more. "What do you want from me?"

The witch turned and left the room, slamming the door. Holly heard her shuffle down the steps. Again, she heard muffled voices, and soon another door slammed and the engine outside started up. Holly's shoulders sagged as whatever vehicle the engine belonged to began to move. Slowly, the sound diminished. She wondered if there was anyone left downstairs. She remained still for five minutes and listened, but the only sounds she heard were the birds chirping outside.

Of course, they'd left her alone. Why else would they need to handcuff her? Sighing, she opened the bag. A peanut butter and jelly sandwich and a bottle of water. *Could be worse.* When she finished eating, she took only a few sips of water. She didn't know when she'd be able to use the bathroom again. She screwed the cap back on the bottle and put it in the bag. Looking toward the window, she noticed the room was starting to darken. Sunset.

She wondered if there was any point in screaming. Why not? Maybe a hiker or a hunter was out there somewhere. "Help!" she screamed as loudly as she could. She repeated shouting the word intermittently every few minutes until she grew hoarse. If the birds heard, they weren't coming to her aid. Was anybody?

33 SEARCH WARRANT

Nick walked into the kitchen, his socks and shoes in his hand. When he sat down, Lucky came over and sat directly in front of him, watching as he put them on.

“So how you been?” Nick smiled and patted the dog on the head. As he started to get up, the dog whimpered and put her paw on his knee. He sat back down and put his hands around the dog’s neck, massaging her ears. “Don’t look so sad.”

When Nick finally stood up, the dog followed him to the door. She whimpered again as he slid open the locks.

“Sorry, Lucky, but you have to stay.” Bending down, he gave her one last pat. “Everything will be all right. I promise.”

As he got in his car, he hoped that was a promise he could keep.

****

An hour later, Nick sat on a plastic chair at the Reddington Manor Police Station. He sipped coffee from a Styrofoam cup as he waited for the arrival of Sheriff Cyrus Bascom. Mary Harris, Bascom’s secretary, glanced up from her keyboard, and cast him a nervous smile. Half an hour had passed since she'd last cautioned him that Bascom might not be in for a while.

Nick returned Mary's smile and appeared to have all the time in the world. Thirty years as a policeman, twenty-five of them as a detective, had taught him patience. At this moment, he felt anything but patient. Although he tried to be as reassuring as he could when he talked to Ivy the night before, he was worried. She was right. Whoever took Holly did not want ransom. She had to have witnessed something that night. He knew of only one sure way to silence a witness.

Nick wanted to stand up and shout at the secretary -- tell her he was here on a matter of life and death -- demand that she get the sheriff on the phone. But his experience had also taught him self-discipline. He knew if he wanted to get any help from this sheriff, he had to appear courteous and respectful. So he sat, sipped his coffee and waited.

Fifteen minutes later the sheriff walked in and strode past Nick. Mary got up and followed him to a desk in the back corner of the one-room office. Nick couldn't hear the exchange between them. Bascom glanced at him, then back at the secretary, nodding slightly.

Returning to her desk, the secretary said, "The sheriff will see you now, Mr. Manelli."

Nick got up and walked over to Bascom. Extending his hand, he said, "Sheriff, I'm Nick Manelli. I'm a detective with the Pineland Park Police Department in New Jersey."

The sheriff raised an eyebrow and shook Nick's hand. "Always a pleasure to meet a fellow law enforcement officer. Have a seat. What can I do for you?"

"Holly Donnelly is my fiancée."

Bascom's eyes widened just a bit and he leaned back in his chair. "I suppose Ms. Farmer called you."

"No, Ivy Donnelly did."

"Oh, right. The sister."

"Sheriff, I'd like to suggest that you get a search warrant for the Leggett house."

Bascom grimaced and looked down at his desk. "Now, Detective, I know that Ms. Farmer has a negative opinion of her neighbor. Why, she's accused him of everything from disturbing the peace to murder, but…"

"Holly saw a man in that house the night before she disappeared. Someone who shut off the light when he saw her…"

"It was the middle of the night." Bascom sniffed. Looking down at his desk, he continued. "You know how women let their imaginations get the best of them. Besides, there's no electricity in…."

"Then whoever she saw had a flashlight or an LED." Nick put his arm on the desk and leaned forward. "If Holly said she saw someone, she saw someone."

Bascom moved his jaw from side to side. "Okay, maybe she did. We have squatters up here, you know. There's no real evidence whoever may or may not have been in the Leggett house had anything to do with Ms. Donnelly's disappearance."

"Is there a reason you don't want to search that house?" Nick asked, stone-faced.

"What are you suggesting?" Bascom sneered, this time looking directly at Nick who stared back, unblinking. After a moment, the sheriff continued. "I assure you, we are doing everything we can to find your intended. "

Nick smiled grimly and after a moment stood up. "Okay, Sheriff." Turning, he headed to the door.

Bascom called after him. "Detective Manelli, I trust you won't try taking the law into your own hands."

Nick stopped beside the secretary's desk and turned slowly to face him. "I'm a lawman, Sheriff. I'd never do that." Looking down at Mary, he said, "The State Police Headquarters I drove past on Route 17 covers this jurisdiction, right?"

Before she could answer, Bascom jumped up from his desk and walked forward. "Just a minute. There's no need to involve the State Police."

"Then get a warrant to search that house," Nick said, steel in his voice.

The beleaguered secretary held her breath as she watched the sheriff and the detective locked in a staring duel. Bascom bit his lower lip. Scowling, he turned to the secretary.

"Mary, get Judge Mallory on the line."

34 THE LEGGETT HOUSE

"Where's Nick? Kate asked as she entered the kitchen.

"I don't know," Ivy replied. "I got up a little after seven. He was gone already." She picked up a piece of paper from the counter. "He just left this note saying 'Back Soon'."

Kate grabbed a mug and poured herself some coffee. "I still think we ought to sneak inside next door and see what's in there."

Ivy rolled her eyes. "I'm going to tell you what I've told Holly dozens of times. Let Nick handle this."

Kate frowned and peered through the window facing Chuck's house. "What's Lucky doing all by herself out in the driveway?"

Ivy stood next to Kate and looked through the window. Lucky lay in front of Holly's car, her head flat on the ground, facing the road.

"When I let the dogs out, she ran right over there, sniffing all around where Nick's car was parked. Except to relieve herself, she hasn't moved. She wouldn't even walk up the road with us."

Kate frowned. "Poor thing. I hadn't thought about how all this was affecting her."

"She was so happy to see Nick when he arrived yesterday. Now, she's probably worried he won't come back either."

Kate stepped back from the window. "Well, the good news is Benny and Razor's truck is in the driveway. I wonder what time they got home last night."

"I have no idea. I tossed and turned for a bit, but once I fell asleep, I didn't open my eyes again until this morning. Do you think they might actually have found out something that could help?" Ivy asked.

"I don't know, but Razor sure seemed to have a destination in mind when he headed out yesterday. We'll just have to wait until they get up."

Ivy sighed. "This waiting is going to kill me." She walked out onto the porch, around to the side facing the Leggett house. Placing her hands on the banister, she stared at the rundown place. The white shingle siding needed a paint job. The red gingerbread trim was peeling. Several window shutters were missing. Two appeared to be hanging by only one nail. The front porch steps had collapsed.

Ivy shook her head. What did that dilapidated structure have to do with Holly's disappearance? But even Nick agreed that the answer to why Holly was abducted lay inside. She felt so much better now that he was here. Still, the situation seemed so hopeless.

"Oh, Holly," she said under her breath. Closing her eyes she prayed that her sister remained safe until they could find her. The sound of a car engine interrupted her thoughts. As the noise grew closer, the dogs ran to the edge of the driveway and began barking.

Ivy hurried across the porch and down the steps as a police cruiser drove past, followed by Nick's car. Kate came running out of the house

"Woo-hoo!" She nudged Ivy. "Looks like you were right. If Nick could get Bascom to get off his butt, he's a god. I will not second guess him again." Starting to jog down the driveway, she said, "C'mon. Let's go."

Ivy smiled and ran to catch up with her. Lucky flew past them, Amy and Winston, close on her heels. They arrived at the Leggett driveway just as Nick got out of his car. He winked at Ivy as the sheriff climbed out of the cruiser and headed to the back door. Kate had already scurried past the police car before Deputy Bascom even opened his door. Ivy waited for him to get out, then followed, stopping next to Kate, just a few feet from the back stoop.

"Try the door," the sheriff said to the deputy. Jason turned the knob and the door opened. He stepped aside allowing the sheriff to enter first. He glanced at Nick, giving him a slight nod, then followed Bascom inside.

Kate started up the single step to the back stoop, but suddenly found herself immobilized, her foot stuck in mid-air. Turning, she jerked her head back and saw that Nick had hold of the back of her sweatshirt jacket.

"Where do you think you're going?" he asked.

"You're kidding, right?" She turned to face him, placing clenched fists on her hips. "After all this, you're not going to let us go inside?"

"That's right." Nick nodded and gave her a droll smile. "This is potentially a crime scene. You wouldn't want to jeopardize the conviction of Boyd Leggett, would you?"

Kate scowled at him. “Hmph. I guess not.” Her shoulders sagged in surrender.

Nick turned to Ivy. “You two stay here.”

Ivy nodded and bit her lip to keep from laughing.

Kate screwed up her mouth and glared at Ivy. “I think I get why Holly broke up with him.”

Unable to hold herself in check any longer, Ivy chuckled. “But you know he’s right, don’t you?”

“I don’t care,” Kate thrust her chest out, her fists still on her hips. “Before Nick Manelli ever arrived, I said we needed to get inside this place. Now the door’s open and I have to stay outside!” Looking down at her feet, she spotted a stone and kicked it into the overgrown grass in the backyard.

Ivy’s smile faded as Jason Bascom came out the back door and ran to the police car. She made eye contact with Kate and together they slowly approached as the deputy pulled out the car phone speaker.

“Mary, call the coroner. Tell him we found a body at the Leggett house.”

35 JAKE

Kate and Ivy watched from Kate's side porch as a State Police car pulled up behind the coroner's van.

"I feel sick." Kate sat forward placing her elbows on her thighs and lowered her head into her hands.

"Let's go inside." Ivy stood up. "Sitting here watching isn't doing anyone any good."

After a moment, Kate lifted her head, tears in her eyes. "All this time, Milly was over there -- dead. I should have done something."

"How could you have known? There was nothing you could have done." Ivy gently tugged on Kate's arm. "C'mon."

Kate got to her feet and Ivy guided her across the porch to the kitchen door, holding the door open for her. Amy and Winston followed her inside, but Lucky stayed put.

"Okay, Lucky," Ivy said. "But you stay on this porch, you hear. Stay."

The dog glanced at Ivy, then lay down facing the Leggett house.

Inside, Ivy asked, “Shall I put on the TV?”

“Why not?” Kate replied, shrugging before she sank into her recliner.

Twenty minutes into a re-run of Frasier, they heard the door open and Nick walked into the living room, Lucky right beside him.

Kate sat up. “Well?”

“They all pretty much acknowledged the body to be Mildred Leggett’s, but they’ll need dental records to confirm her identity. In addition to the body, they found stolen goods and fifty one ounce packets of what they believe to be marijuana. They have to test to confirm that, too.”

“What happens next?” Kate asked.

“The State Police have issued an APB for Boyd Leggett.”

“But are they out there looking for him?” Ivy stood up. “And what about Holly? Are they looking for her? You aren’t going to just sit here and wait, are you?”

Nick just shook his head in reply. “Kate, have you heard from the guys next door?”

Kate jumped up. “I forgot all about them. If they’re not up yet, let’s go wake them.” She made a beeline for the door without looking back.

Nick waited for Ivy. As she drew near, he put an arm around her.

“I’m sorry,” she said looking up at him.

“For what?” he asked as they walked into the kitchen.

“I know better than to think you’d just sit around and wait.”

"Forget about it," he said, squeezing her shoulder and opening the door for her.

As they crossed the yard, they could hear Kate pounding on Chuck's back door. After a few minutes, a bleary-eyed Benny greeted them.

"What time is it?" he asked.

"Eleven thirty," Kate replied, as she pushed past him into the kitchen.

Benny held the door for Ivy and Nick.

Ivy smiled at Benny. "This is Detective Nick Manelli."

Benny's eyes widened. "Detective?"

"He's Holly's..."

"Fiancé," Nick said when she hesitated.

Benny shook the hand Nick offered him. "Oh, man. I'm really sorry."

"Benny," Kate cut in, "they found Milly Leggett's body in the house next door."

"What! No way." Benny shook his head in disbelief. "First, Chuck, now Milly. This is messed up."

"Did you and Razor find out anything yesterday?" Ivy asked.

"Oh -- yeah. I almost forgot. Let me go get Razor. He'll tell you."

As they heard Benny mount the stairs, Kate held up both her hands, fingers crossed. Only a few minutes passed before they heard footsteps descending the stairs.

"You must be Razor," Nick said, extending his hand as the big man entered the room.

Razor nodded and shook Nick's hand. "I'm waiting for a call back." He glanced down at the cellphone in his hand, then back up at Nick. "Boyd's girlfriend, Roxy Barnett, has a sister, Earline. I know Earline's old boyfriend, Jake. That's who we went looking for last night. We went to the bar where he used to hang. He wasn't there, but I got his new phone number. I called last night and left a message." He looked down at his phone again. "Still no return call."

"How do you think this guy can help?" Nick asked.

"Years ago the four of them used to throw parties at an abandoned house on a property owned by the Barnetts. I never went to one, but I was thinking maybe Boyd's got Holly there."

Nick nodded. "Can you try calling this guy again?"

Razor turned on the phone and tapped the screen. "Jake? Razor." The hulk of a man smiled. "Never mind that. Listen, I remember you and Earline used to throw parties out in the woods. Can you tell me how to get there?" Razor laughed. "Uh-huh…uh-huh. Thanks, man. I owe you."

The smile left Razor's face as he disconnected and looked from Nick to Benny. "Let's roll."

36 BREADCRUMB

"Nick! How did you find me?"

He just stood in the doorway smiling.

"I'm so sorry -- for everything. I was so wrong to break up with you. Can you forgive me?"

Nick didn't move. He remained standing in the doorway as the smile faded from his face.

"Aren't you going to untie me?" Holly asked, looking at the rope that bound her wrist to the bedpost. *Wait a minute. Wasn't that a handcuff before?*

Nick walked over to the bed, an ugly sneer on his face. He pushed her shoulder roughly.

"Get up!"

Holly felt a punch to her upper arm and blinked. As her eyes focused she realized the figure standing beside the bed was the witch -- not Nick Manelli.

"What do you want?" Holly asked, covering her face with her hands. Suddenly she realized she was no longer cuffed to the bed.

"Get up."

"Why?"

"Just get up." The masked woman grasped her arm and pulled her to her feet. She dragged Holly to the bathroom and thrust her inside. "Hurry up."

Holly glanced at herself in the mirror as she undid her shorts. Her hair was beginning to look like a bird's nest. When she was just about finished, the door shook on its hinges.

"Are you done yet?"

"Shut up," Holly replied as she pulled up her zipper. She sighed wearily as the slight stream of water coming out of the tap slowly covered her hands. Reaching behind her, she stuck her hands in her back pockets to dry them, and felt something in the right-side pocket. Pulling it out, she saw it was her college business card. When was the last time she'd worn these shorts? And how did this card survive a trip through the washing machine? After another loud bang on the door, she quickly slid the card back in her pocket and smiled grimly into the mirror. *At least they'll be able to identify you when they find your body.*

"About time," the witch said when Holly opened the door and stepped into the hallway. As Holly walked past her and headed back to the bedroom, the woman again grabbed her arm. This time she twisted it behind her back and pinned her up against the wall. The witch's bony elbow held her in place. Grasping Holly's other arm, she pulled it behind her back as well. Holly felt rope circling her wrists.

"What's going on?" Holly grimaced as her captor pulled the ropes tightly.

"Just walk," she said and pushed Holly to the stairs.

A little off balance with her hands behind her, Holly moved slowly, leaning on the banister as she started downward.

"Move it!" The witch grabbed her arm and pulled. Holly was actually grateful for the steadying effect of the woman's grip on her. She surveyed the downstairs room as they descended. A well-worn couch and armchair were the only furnishings. She was able to see partially through an arched doorway to the back door of what she thought must be the kitchen. The storm door was open and she could see through an old-fashioned wood-framed screen door to the outside.

When they reached the bottom of the stairs, the witch pushed Holly down into the arm chair, blindfolded her and then walked away. Holly heard the screen open and slam, then nothing else but the birds. She wondered what the witch and whoever she was working with had in store for her.

If they were going to kill her, they could have done it already. Were they taking her somewhere else to murder her. But why? They clearly were miles from anywhere and this place was not lived in. It would take forever for anyone to find her.

A motor engine interrupted her thoughts. The sound grew louder, until the vehicle came to a stop. A car door opened and slammed shut again. Holly heard a man's voice. She sat as quietly as she could, straining to hear. She even held her breath, but still couldn't make out what was being said.

Suddenly, she heard the man's voice shout. "Dammit. Let's go. They could be on their way here now."

Holly's pulse spiked. Someone must be looking for her. As she heard the screen door squeak open, she lifted her arms up slightly to reach into her back pocket. Sliding her index finger and thumb inside, she pulled out the business card, then slumped down, stuffing it in the crevice between the cushion and chair arm. As footsteps came nearer, she sat up straight and held her breath.

The witch's now familiar voice barked, "Get up," as she grabbed Holly by the arm and again pulled her to her feet.

As she was dragged across the room, Holly finally exhaled. The witch hadn't spotted the card. Would anyone else discover the breadcrumb she'd left behind?

37 EVIDENCE

“So, I didn’t know Holly was engaged,” Benny said, turning slightly to face Nick, as he sat in the crew cab seat of the Silverado. “She wasn’t wearing a ring.”

When Nick didn’t reply, Benny guffawed. “Oh, I get it. She doesn’t believe in symbols of baggage, right?”

“That’s bondage.” Razor shook his head. “Just ignore him,” he said, glancing at Nick in the rear view mirror.

“C’mon, man,” Benny said sheepishly. “I was just trying to make conversation.”

“How far is this place?” Nick asked looking out the window.

“About five miles,” Razor replied, shooting Benny a look of warning.

Benny frowned, sinking down in his seat. They drove in silence until Razor slowed down. “The turnoff should be coming up soon.” After another hundred yards, he said, “Here it is.”

Nick squinted as he watched the big man make a right hand turn into what appeared to be a solid, green wall. As the branches parted and they reached a clearing, he made a note to ask later how Razor knew where to turn.

Now moving on a dirt road, Razor slowed down to a crawl. The Silverado rocked a bit as he maneuvered his way across the rutted path. He continued about a quarter mile, when Nick said, “Stop. How much further do you think it is?”

“Jake said the house was about three-quarters of a mile from the road.”

“I want to walk the rest of the way in,” Nick said, opening the door and climbing out of the truck.

By the time Razor shut off the engine and he and Benny got out, they had to run to catch up with Nick.

“He must really love her,” Benny whispered to Razor.

Nick never slowed down until the house came into view. He surveyed the ramshackle building and its surroundings. No vehicles in sight, but he knew that didn’t mean no one was inside. Razor and Benny came up behind him just as he reached inside his jacket to his shoulder holster and pulled out his gun.

“Okay. You two stay here.”

Before either could reply, Nick bent low and moved quickly along the overgrown weeds towards the house. Benny started to follow, but Razor held him back. “Didn’t I teach you? You always listen to the man with the gun.”

Nick reached the corner of the house and crouched low, moving across the porch below the windows. When he reached the door, in one fluid motion he stood up, kicked it in and entered the house. After a few minutes, he reappeared on the porch and waved the two men over.

Nick holstered his gun and walked back into the house. Benny and Razor followed.

"There's garbage in here," Nick said as he looked down at a waste can filled with paper bags, soda cans and beer bottles. "But this could have been here for months."

Benny came up alongside Nick and peered down at the trash. "Nuh-uh," he said reaching down and rooting through the bags and cans. Pulling out a plastic cup with a straw in the lid, he sniffed it. Smiling he turned to Nick. "This is a McDonald's Cherry Berry Chiller cup. I recognize the smell. It's a new drink they just introduced last week." With the air of a forensics specialist, Benny pointed to the waste bin and declared, "This garbage is recent."

Nick stared at Benny for a moment, then glanced over at Razor.

"He knows his fast food," the big guy said, the corners of his mouth twitching.

"Okay," Nick said heading to the stairs. "I just raced through before. Let's take a closer look and see if there's anything else -- any evidence -- that could help us determine who was here."

Each of the men took a bedroom. After a few minutes they met back in the hallway.

"Nothing?" Nick asked. Benny and Razor shook their heads.

Nick stepped into the bathroom and gave a quick look around. Had Holly been here, he wondered. Or, was coming here just a wild goose chase after all? Still, he felt Razor's instincts had been on target. And, after what they'd found in the Leggett house, he was sure Boyd Leggett was responsible for Holly's disappearance. Wherever he was, Holly was with him -- if she was still…

“Nick! We found something,” Razor yelled up the stairs.

Nick flew down the steps. Benny held up a small piece of paper, grinning as if he were holding the winning lottery ticket. Nick took it from him. An adrenaline rush coursed through his veins as he recognized Holly’s business card.

Razor tapped his shoulder. “She was here, man.”

Nick closed his eyes and nodded. *She’s alive.*

38 ON THE MOVE

Ivy refilled the chickens' water dishes as Kate collected eggs in a basket. Together they cleaned the coop and spread the feed. Amy and Winston lay in the grass just outside the coop.

When they finished, Kate put the rake away and picked up the basket. "Okay," she said. "What do you say to omelets for dinner?"

"Fine by me." Ivy looked to the corner of the yard opposite the chicken coop. "I meant to tell you the other day that your rose arbor is gorgeous."

"Yeah." Kate's expression turned dreamy as she gazed at the arbor laden with rosebuds, not yet in bloom. "I planted those roses after my daughter was born. I thought it would be the perfect spot for her wedding." Sliding the latch on the chicken coop door, she frowned. "So far she hasn't found Mr. Right."

"She's young," Ivy said as they headed back to the house. "Look how long it took Holly to find Mr. Right."

"You think they can work things out?" Kate asked.

Ivy raised her chin. "Yes, I do. Now that I know *she* broke it off with Nick, I'll hold those cold feet of hers to the fire until she…" Ivy broke off, her look of determination fading.

Kate gave Ivy's shoulder a reassuring pat. "Nick will find her. In the meantime, I wish there was something we could do for *her*." Kate tipped her head in the direction of Lucky who had once again taken up her sentry post near the driveway.

"I know. I think she's really missing Holly." Ivy sighed.

"C'mon," Kate frowned. "It's too hot to garden, so I guess we'll just have to play gin rummy on the porch until Nick gets back."

"Okay. But, I swear, if we don't hear from him soon, I'm going to start knocking on doors and searching for Holly myself -- house by house -- barn by barn."

Kate laughed. "That's not a bad idea."

As they reached the porch, they stopped at the sound of a car coming up the road.

"It's only Flo," Kate said as Flo's Kia pulled into the driveway.

"Where the hell is Benny?" she bellowed as she got out of the car.

"It's a long story," Kate said, waving Flo over. "Come have some iced tea, and we'll catch you up on what's been happening."

****

"Hot damn!" the big woman said when Kate finished describing the events of the last two days. She gazed over at her car. "And after I told Cyrus to haul that worthless sack of …"

"Flo," Kate cut in, "do you mind my asking why the sheriff's so protective of Boyd?"

Flo stared at Kate a moment, then dropped her gaze to the porch floor. "I don't really know."

Kate bit her lip, realizing the mistake she'd made by asking a direct question. Whatever relationship Flo had with Cyrus, she wasn't sharing.

The sound of the phone ringing broke the silence and Ivy jumped up and ran inside. Kate stood up and remained by the screen door listening.

Ivy wiped tears away as she stepped back outside. "They found Holly's business card at that abandoned farmhouse. Nick's on his way to the sheriff's office."

Kate let out a deep sigh. "Razor was right." Turning to Flo, she said, "Maybe you ought to recommend that Sheriff Bascom hire him."

Flo sneered and waved her hand dismissively. After a moment she leaned back, musing, "This means Boyd definitely has your friend." Her brow furrowed as she looked up at the sky. "And he's on the move."

Kate and Ivy exchanged a glance. This time Kate knew better than to ask any questions. Ivy sank down onto a chair.

"I wonder if Razor knows of any other hideouts Boyd might go to," she said, looking down at her hands.

The crease left Flo's brow. "I do. I'd bet money that low-life is on his way to Sonny Telicky's mother's place."

"Where's that?" Ivy moved to the edge of her chair.

"Near the lake. Kate, you know that dirt road about a mile past the Inn?" Flo asked.

"Yeah, I think so," Kate replied.

"It's off that road," she nodded. "Yep, I bet that's where he goes next."

All three women looked across the lawn as a beat-up GMC Gremlin pulled into the driveway behind Flo's car. Barbara and Ashley got out and waved.

"Gotta go." Flo struggled up out of her chair. "We got some people coming to look at Chuck's tools. See ya's later," she said as she lumbered down the steps.

Ivy stood up. "Do you know how to get to this place she's talking about?"

Kate nodded. "Yeah, I'm pretty sure I do."

"Then let's get the dogs in the house and go."

Kate grabbed her by the arm. "Hold on a second. It's my turn to be cautious," she said. "Shouldn't we wait for Nick?"

"I'll call him on the way, but we need to go now. If Flo's right and Boyd's on the move, we don't have a minute to lose."

39 SHOWDOWN

As Razor pulled into a parking space in front of the police station, he looked in the rearview mirror at Nick.

"I think Benny and me should stay in the truck."

Benny turned to Nick. "Yeah, he's right. Bascom's made escape goats out of us before and for no reason."

"That's scapegoats, Benny," Razor corrected.

"That's what I said." Benny gave his friend a look of exasperation. Glancing back at Nick, he continued. "If it wasn't for Aunt Flo, I think he'd find a way to lock us up and throw away the key."

Nick got out of the truck and entered the police station. He nodded at Mary Harris who started to say something, then just stared at him as he strode past her over to where Sheriff Bascom sat talking on the phone. The sheriff frowned as his eyes met Nick's.

"I'll have to call you back," he said, replacing the phone in its cradle. "Not sure what the protocol is in New Jersey, Detective, but up here it's customary to wait to be announced before bursting in on the sheriff."

Ignoring the comment, Nick put Holly's card on the desk. "I found this card in an abandoned farmhouse."

Bascom sat staring at the card for a moment. When he finally looked up, he squinted at Nick, a grim smile on his face. "Now, are you telling me you trespassed on private property? I cautioned you before about taking the law into your own hands."

Nick looked down at Bascom, again not taking the bait. In a calm voice he continued. "This is evidence that Holly was in that house, a house that belongs to the family of Boyd Leggett's girlfriend, the Barnetts."

The sheriff leaned back in his chair. His furrowed brow reduced his eyes to mere slits. "Now, how in the world would you know that?"

Not replying to the question, Nick met the sheriff's glare with an emotionless expression. After several uncomfortable moments, the sheriff sat forward and picked up Holly's business card. At the sound of the front door opening, Bascom looked up appearing relieved to see his deputy walk in. When Jason Bascom spotted Nick, he hesitated. Mary gave him a wide-eyed look and a helpless shrug of her shoulders.

"Jason, come over here." The elder Bascom stood up and walked past Nick to where the deputy stood. "You want to take the detective's statement? He thinks he's found some evidence." He handed the deputy the business card, then peered through the front windows at the Silverado.

"Detective, don't tell me you're operating on the advice of those two circus freaks out there," Bascom scoffed.

Nick turned to face Bascom. "Those two circus freaks have demonstrated superior instincts resulting in the first break in the investigation of Holly Donnelly's disappearance, Sheriff. In fact, you might want to consider hiring them."

Bascom glowered at Nick. "Just who the hell.."

Nick turned to the deputy. "I found that card you're holding at a farmhouse owned by the Barnetts. Roxy Barnett is Boyd Leggett's girlfriend. The place should be dusted for fingerprints. That's my statement."

The sheriff blocked Nick's path as he headed to the door. "You don't tell my deputy what should or should not be done."

Nick got as close to Bascom as possible without touching the man. Six inches taller, he bent his head downward and growled, "And *you* don't tell me what to do." Just above a whisper, he added, "When this is over, I'm going to find the connection between you and Boyd Leggett."

The sheriff jerked his head back, a brief look of alarm stealing across his face.

Nick turned and walked out the door. Outside, Razor stood on the sidewalk. They exchanged a glance, then got in the truck.

As Razor turned the key in the ignition, Benny said, "Things looked tense in there, man. Razor thought you might need back up."

"I appreciate that. You guys just let me deal with the cops."

"Where to?" Razor asked as he pulled away from the curb.

"Kate's place." Nick pulled out his phone and saw there was a message from Ivy. He hit playback and listened. "Damn!"

"What's the matter?" Benny asked.

"Do you know how to get to Sonny Telicky's mother's place?"

40 RESCUE

Holly woke up, her head throbbing. She blinked looking up at a shaft of sunlight streaming through an opening high above her. She tried to sit up and found her wrist once again handcuffed to something behind her. Twisting her head she saw she was now chained to a metal wheel. As her eyes came into focus in the dimly lit space, she realized she was in a barn. *Great. Just great.*

Slowly, she sidled up the wheel until she was in a sitting position. She strained to listen for any sound to help figure out where they dumped her this time. Again, not even the distant hum of traffic -- just birds chirping. When this was over, she was never visiting farm country or the woods again. Kate would just have to come to Pineland Park if she wanted to see her -- that is, if she ever got back to New Jersey.

With her free hand, she rubbed her forehead. What had they given her to cause this pounding headache? And where were they? The last thing she remembered was being hustled into some kind of vehicle. Was it a van? An SUV? She couldn't be sure. And how did they drug her? She couldn't remember drinking or eating anything. *What difference does it make anyway?*

Suddenly she remembered. Somebody was looking for her. That's why they were moving her. *"They could be on their way here now."* That's what the man shouted before the witch came and dragged her out of the house.

Who was the "they" they were talking about? How long had it been since she was kidnapped, she wondered. Was it long enough for them to initiate a missing person search? Was the sheriff looking for her? She couldn't see him putting in much effort to find her.

Or was it Kate and Ivy? But how would they have ever figured out where she was? She smiled as she imagined her sister and her friend asking the tarot cards where they could find her. What card would let them know she was chained to a wheel in a barn?

Wait a minute! Would Ivy call Nick? If she did, would he come?

A sound on the other side of the barn interrupted her thoughts. *What was that? Oh, please just be a field mouse.* Then she saw it. A snake.

Holly gasped and her heart started racing. She held her breath and tried not to move as she watched the reptile slither across the floor towards her. All of her nightmares about snakes had not been nearly as terrifying as this moment. A bead of sweat ran down the side of her face. She screamed, but the snake kept coming in her direction. Was this it? Was this how she was going to die? She closed her eyes and screamed again.

Suddenly, the door of the barn flew open and sunlight came flooding in. A young man ran in, spotted the snake and quickly grabbed a shovel leaning against the wall. Bringing the sharp edge down, he dissected the reptile just a few inches in front of Holly.

"Are you okay?" he asked.

Holly panted as if she'd crossed the finish line of a hundred-yard dash. She just nodded. As her rescuer knelt beside her, she finally managed to croak out, "Thank you."

Examining the handcuff, the young man asked, "Who handcuffed you here?"

"I don't know. A woman -- and a man. They wore masks. I was at a farmhouse -- I don't know how long. Then I woke up here." Holly's brow creased as she tried to make sense out of what she'd been through. Finally, she looked at the sandy-haired young fellow in front of her and asked, "Who are you?"

"Tommy Cranston. Who are you?"

Holly stared at him a moment, her mouth slightly open. Shaking her head, she smiled at him. "I'm Holly Donnelly, Kate Farmer's friend.

"Oh, boy." Tommy stood up and started searching around the barn. "The man and woman were probably Boyd Leggett and his girlfriend. "We've got to get you loose and get out of here."

As Tommy poked around and turned things over, Holly asked, "How did you find me? Were you looking for me?"

"No. I was planning to sleep in this barn tonight, and thought I'd come in and check it out before dark. Just as I got here, I heard you scream."

"Lucky for me," Holly said, glancing at the dead reptile. "Is that a poisonous snake?"

"Yeah, it's a copperhead."

"Would I have died if it bit me?"

"Probably not, but you'd have been in a world of hurt." Tommy smiled. "Nothing Kate couldn't have healed with something growing in her back yard."

Holly laughed. "You know her well."

"Here we go." Tommy held up a hammer. "This might work." He bent to examine the cuffs, then ran his hand along the rusty spoke of the wheel. Kneeling down, he said, "I'm going to try to pound the spoke loose. Close your eyes."

Holly squeezed her eyes shut and turned her head away as the hammer made contact with the metal. After four loud bangs, the spoke pulled away from the wheel. Tommy slid the cuff off the spoke and helped Holly to her feet.

"C'mon," he said, dropping the hammer.

Holly staggered.

"Can you walk?" he asked, a concerned look on his face as he grasped her elbow.

Holly moved forward cautiously. After a step or two, she replied, "Yeah."

Just as she started moving forward, they both heard it at the same time -- an engine.

"We've got to run," Tommy urged, tugging on her arm.

Holly pushed Tommy away. "I can't run," she said. "You'll just get caught. Go get help."

Tommy hesitated a moment, but realized she was right. "I'll let them know where you are." He squeezed her arm and was gone, closing the door behind him.

Holly sank down onto the floor wondering how she was going to explain the snake.

41 THE TELICKY HOUSE

"Can't you drive any faster?" Ivy let out an impatient sigh.

"No. I'm not your sister." Kate frowned. "Try calling Nick again," she said as she slowed down for a curve in the road.

Ivy hit redial. "Still going straight to message. Maybe he's in a 'no service' zone."

"Or maybe Bascom's thrown him in jail."

Ivy shook her head. "Don't worry about that. Nick knows how to handle Bascom. I have complete faith in him."

They drove in silence for another mile when the lake came into view. "There are only a few roads off this side of the lake," Kate said. "I'm going to slow down even more. Watch for turnoffs."

Ivy gripped the armrest and sat forward. After a quarter mile, she spotted an opening. "Is this one coming up?"

"Yes, but I know the house up there. It's not the Telicky's."

After another half-mile, Ivy again said, "What about here?"

Kate checked her rearview mirror. No one behind her. She brought the car to a complete stop and peered past Ivy through the passenger side window.

"I'm pretty sure this is it."

She turned onto the gravel road and proceeded slowly into the wooded area. She hadn't driven more than a few yards, when Ivy put her hand on her forearm.

"Stop," Ivy said. "Maybe we shouldn't drive right up to the house. Maybe it would be better if we sneak up on them."

Kate nodded. "You're right." She turned off the ignition and removed the keys.

Ivy got out of the car and started walking up the gravel road.

"Wait," Kate said in a stage whisper. She waved Ivy back. Opening the trunk, she poked around. "Here," she said, handing Ivy an umbrella. Ivy rolled her eyes, but took the umbrella anyway.

Next, Kate picked up a large flashlight and slammed the trunk shut. Reopening her car door, she rooted around in her handbag. "Put this in your pocket." She handed Ivy a fingernail file and slipped a pair of cuticle clippers in her pocket.

Together the two women headed up the gravel path. Within a few minutes, they spotted a log cabin. A rusty Ford pick-up and a mud-spattered Jeep sat parked in front.

"I'm not so sure about this," Kate said. "Maybe we should go back and wait for Nick. If we just sit in the car blocking the road out, they can't get away."

Ivy took a deep breath. "Go ahead. You go back to the car. Try redialing Nick."

Kate jerked her head back like a cartoon character. "And leave you to go up there alone?"

Ivy just nodded.

"No way."

"Okay then. Let's try sneaking around the back of the place and see if we can peek in the windows." Ivy took the lead using the umbrella to part the bushes.

Shaking her head, Kate followed. When they arrived directly behind the cabin, Ivy pulled Kate to a crouching position. "You stay here."

Before Kate could object, Ivy scurried across the overgrown patch of crabgrass to a window at the left of the backdoor. Standing on tiptoe, she cupped her eyes and looked inside. Stepping back she moved past the back door and walked up to the window on the right. Again, she peeked in. Turning, she scurried back to where Kate waited.

"I heard voices, but no one is in those bedrooms."

"Let's go then." Kate started to stand up.

Ivy grabbed her wrist, pulling her back down to a kneeling position. "Wait. That doesn't mean she's not in there. I'm not leaving until I'm sure."

"Can I help you, ladies?" a man's voice came from behind them.

Together the women stood up and turned to face a bear of a man. Ivy would later say that if you looked mountain man up in the dictionary, you would find this man's picture. Tall, dark and grisly. Clad in oil stained jeans and a flannel shirt, he held a shotgun under his arm. His black hair was slicked straight back and reached his shoulders. He needed a shave and shower.

Ivy licked her lips and gave him a weak smile. "We were just hiking and got lost. When we spotted the cabin, we were just debating whether we should go knock and ask directions."

"Expecting rain?" Mountain Man asked, eyeing the umbrella in Ivy's hand.

"Well, you never know." She shrugged sheepishly.

"Hiking in the daylight carrying a heavy flashlight, too." A menacing grin crossed his face as he looked at Kate. "Let's go inside," he said, pointing the barrel of the shotgun up to the cabin.

"Really, if you could just point us in the direction of the lake highway, we'll be fine," Kate said.

The man said nothing, but kept the gun pointed at the cabin. Kate and Ivy started walking.

"Are you Sonny Telicky?" Ivy asked.

Again, the grizzled man did not reply. When they reached the front of the cabin, a skinny, bald man, not anywhere near as big as Mountain Man, stood with one haunch resting on the porch railing. "Doesn't look like you got us any supper," he guffawed. "I guess we'll just have to settle for dessert." The corners of his mouth turned upward in a malicious grin. Mountain Man chuckled in reply and rested the shotgun in the crook of his arm.

During the amused interchange between the greasy pair, Ivy made eye contact with Kate and got a tight grip on the umbrella. With all the strength she could muster, she swung it upward, knocking the shotgun out of Mountain Man's arm.

"Run," she yelled unnecessarily. Kate was already sprinting down the gravel path. Ivy raced behind her as a volley of curses trailed after them. Rounding a curve in the road, they saw their car, but they could hear the men gaining on them. When the skinnier of the pair got close, he lunged at Ivy, knocking her to the ground. Kate spun around and swung the flashlight. She made contact with his forehead causing him to release his grip.

Before Kate could help Ivy get back on her feet, Mountain Man had caught up with them. She prepared to swing the flashlight again, but to her surprise, the big man took a step backward.

"That's right. Back up, pal," a voice behind them said.

The women turned to see Nick pointing his hand gun at the man. Razor walked over and helped Ivy to her feet.

"What the hell, Sonny?" Benny placed his hands on his hips. "This is what you do for kicks now?

Sonny just scowled in reply as his friend struggled to stand up, rubbing the bump on his forehead.

Once Razor had Ivy upright, he jogged past everyone up to the cabin.

"Have you seen Boyd?" Benny asked as Nick kept his gun aimed at Sonny.

"Boyd? No, I ain't seen him and I probably won't unless I go looking for him. He owes me money."

Benny just nodded.

"Look, these gals came snooping around my cabin. That's trespass."

"You want us to call the sheriff for you?" Nick asked.

As Sonny bit his lip and shook his head, Razor came back into view. He made eye contact with Nick and just shook his head. Nick lowered his gun and turned to Ivy and Kate.

"Are you okay?" he asked, looking concerned. "Can you drive?"

"Yeah, sure," Kate said. Ivy just nodded.

"Good," he said, his concerned expression turning less sympathetic. "Because we're going to have a little talk when we get back."

42 A SURPRISE CALL

"But I did call you, Nick -- three times," Ivy said.

Nick looked up at the kitchen ceiling, took a deep breath, then turned to Kate.

"Don't look at me," she said in reply to his glare." I told her we should wait for you."

"She did." Ivy sighed.

Nick walked to the window and stood staring out back for a moment. Kate looked at Ivy and mouthed, "Told you so."

When Nick turned back to face them, he appeared calmer. "I can't worry about you and search for Holly at the same time. I'm gonna say this just once. Under absolutely no circumstances are you two to go off alone. Is that clear?"

"Crystal." Kate nodded.

"Clear," Ivy replied. "Sorry, Nick."

He left them sitting in the kitchen as he stepped out onto the porch, Lucky right on his heels. Benny and Razor stood waiting at the bottom of the steps.

"Anything you want us to do, Nick?" Benny asked.

Nick walked down the steps and tilted his head in the direction of the driveway. The tattooed pair followed him. Once out of earshot of the house, he began. "Ivy said your Aunt Flo suggested Boyd would go to Sonny Telicky's. Could you call her and see if she knows anyone or any other place he might go for help?"

"Sure, I can do that," Benny replied.

"Good. Now, go get some sleep. We can start again in the morning -- and thanks. You guys have been a big help. I appreciate it."

Razor just nodded. Benny smiled. "Hey, man, no problem.

Nick returned to the porch and sank down into a wicker chair. Lucky sat and dropped her head on his knee. Resting his hand on the dog's head, he stared at the darkening sky wondering what his next move was. He honestly didn't know.

Without help from the police, he had to rely on information from the locals. He had no way of knowing if he could trust them either. Benny and Razor had proven themselves, not just trustworthy, but helpful. Conversely, Flo's lead put Ivy and Kate in danger. Sonny Telicky was on the outs with Boyd. Had Flo known that?

The only good thing that came out of today was learning that Holly was alive. But that left him with a question that troubled him all day. Why was she still alive? If she had witnessed something, why hadn't Boyd already murdered her?

After 30 years in law enforcement, he knew some petty criminals drew the line at killing. Theft and drug deals didn't warrant the same penalties as murder. Some thieves didn't even carry weapons because armed robbery carried much longer prison sentences than simple theft.

But why was Holly being held hostage? It didn't make sense. That was the question he couldn't answer. Unless Boyd just needed her out of the way until -- until what? Until he could get away? Until he did one more job? Until he got his mother's body out of the house? *Damn!* If that was it and Boyd found out they'd already discovered the body, would there be any reason to keep Holly alive? They were running out of time.

Nick's phone chirped and he looked down at the screen. A number he didn't recognize.

"Manelli," he answered.

"This is Deputy Bascom, detective. I need to talk to you."

43 A PROMISE

Ivy looked out the window to where Nick stood talking to Benny and Razor. "I guess going to Sonny Telicky's was a stupid thing to do."

"Yeah," Kate agreed. After a moment she chuckled. "But you have to admit the umbrella and flashlight came in handy. I'm just glad the guys showed up before we had to use the cuticle clippers."

Ivy shook her head smiling. "You really are crazy." She continued watching out the window as Nick turned back to the porch and sat down.

"Let's go in the living room," she whispered. Sitting down on the couch she said, "What can we do to help him?"

"Unfortunately, the only thing we can do is the hardest thing of all -- just wait." Kate picked up the deck of cards on the table. "Gin rummy?"

Ivy let out a resigned sigh. "Why not?"

In the middle of the first hand, Nick walked in. "I have to go out."

"Where?" Ivy asked. "Can we go with you?"

"No."

"But you're going to tell us where you're going, aren't you?" Kate lay her cards down on the table.

"Yeah, we worry about you, too," Ivy said, standing up.

After a moment, Nick replied. "I'm going to the Stillwell Taphouse."

"That's ten miles from here." Kate's brow creased.

"Why are you going there?" Ivy asked

"Deputy Bascom asked to meet me there."

"I don't think you should go alone." Ivy took a step closer to him.

"You're not going." Nick gave her an indulgent smile.

"Why don't you get Benny and Razor to go with you?" Kate suggested.

"Yes, that's a great idea," Ivy said.

"I'm going alone and I want you both to promise you won't leave this house while I'm gone," Nick said.

Ivy grunted in exasperation. "Okay, I promise, but I'm going to call you every thirty minutes until you get back here."

"Fine," Nick said turning to Kate. "Now, let me hear you say it."

Kate twisted her mouth and finally said, "I promise not to leave the house while you're gone. Okay? Happy?"

Nick just nodded and headed to the kitchen, Ivy, Kate and Lucky following him. At the door, he looked down at the dog. "You stay, too, Lucky."

The forlorn dog just watched as Nick stepped out onto the porch. "Lock this door," he said and was gone.

Kate twisted the deadbolt and turned to face Ivy. "You know, more and more, I'm beginning to understand why Holly broke up with him."

"Oh, c'mon. You know he's right." Ivy frowned. "At least, I hope he is tonight." She looked out the window as he backed his car down the driveway. "I don't like him going out alone. What's he thinking? Don't cops always want back-up."

"We can follow him." Kate waggled her eyebrows.

"You just promised you wouldn't leave the house!"

"Don't tell me you didn't cross your fingers." Kate pursed her lips.

Ivy sighed. "I don't believe you."

An impish grin spread across Kate's face and she snapped her fingers. "We'll fix him." She picked up her cellphone and tapped in a number.

"Benny. It's Kate. I need a favor."

44 STILLWELL TAPHOUSE

Nick pulled into a parking space in front of the Stillwell Taphouse. Only a handful of vehicles, mostly pick-ups and SUV's were scattered across the lot. No police car. As he turned off the ignition, his phone chirped. He looked at the screen and shook his head.

"I just got here, Ivy. Yeah, I'm alive and well. Good-bye," he said and disconnected.

Inside the dimly lit tavern, Nick surveyed the circular bar backed by a glass wall displaying a row of gleaming brewery fermenters. A half-dozen patrons sat with their eyes focused on either the wide-screen TV or the drinks in front of them. Deputy Bascom was not one of them. No one but the bartender even glanced up as Nick took a step closer to the bar.

To the left of the bar, not a soul was seated at a row of tables beneath a trophy wall. Antlers of every horned animal in the Catskills filled the wall, along with a smattering of plaques with stuffed trout mounted on them. Turning to his right, Nick spotted Jason Bascom seated alone in a back booth and headed in his direction.

Out of uniform, the policeman appeared younger than he had this morning at the Leggett house. Nick judged him to be in his late thirties, maybe early forties. Clad in blue jeans and a Buffalo Bills Tee-shirt, he looked like any other patron of this backwoods bar.

"Thanks for coming," he said extending his hand. "Have a seat."

Nick shook the offered hand, slid into the booth and waited.

Bascom made eye contact with Nick, then looked down at the beer mug in front of him. Lifting the mug, he downed the remaining contents and waved the bartender over.

"Another Stillwell Pale Ale," he said, then looked at Nick.

"The same," Nick replied.

Jason leaned against the back of the booth. "The coroner says he's pretty sure after his initial examination that Milly Leggett died of natural causes and that she's probably been dead for three months."

When Nick just nodded, Jason continued. "We checked with her bank. Her social security checks and pension have continued to be deposited during those three months, and withdrawals have been made from ATM's in Monticello."

The young policeman paused, raking his fingers through his dirty blond hair. "We've requested bank security videos. We're pretty certain they'll confirm that Boyd Leggett made those withdrawals."

Nick smiled. "You didn't ask me to drive ten miles out of town just to tell me this. Why am I here?"

As the bartender returned and placed a frosted mug of beer in front of each of them, Jason eyed

Nick, a look of uncertainty on his face. When the bartender left, he inhaled deeply, placed his arms on the table and leaned toward Nick.

"I went out to the Barnett place and dusted for fingerprints like you suggested. Boyd was definitely there. I also have a friend who works at the county forensics lab. She told me she tested two of the fifty marijuana samples we took from the Leggett house. She said they were pure oregano."

"Unless Boyd was planning on opening an Italian restaurant, sounds like somebody switched them," Nick said.

"Had to," Jason replied.

"Why you telling me this?

"Look, I know what my uncle says, but the evidence shows Boyd's got your fiancée. Boyd's also running drugs."

"Do you think he murdered Chuck Dwyer?" Nick asked.

"No." Jason shook his head. "By the way, my forensics friend also told me Chuck was unconscious when whoever murdered him, put that meat cleaver in his chest. Blow to the back of the head with a blunt instrument."

"So they knocked him out, then bludgeoned him and left him there to bleed out. Why don't you think it was Boyd?" Nick asked.

"I know Boyd. He's a petty criminal, but I don't think he's a killer -- but whoever is running interference for him …" Jason paused.

"You can't say the same about them." Nick finished the sentence and took a sip of beer.

Jason just nodded.

The two men sat in silence for a while. Finally, Nick spoke. "Seems like whoever switched the marijuana must work in law enforcement." He lifted the beer to his lips and took a long swallow.

Jason glanced down at his beer and took a deep breath. "Look. I just want to help you find Ms. Donnelly,"

Nick nodded. "How do you propose to do that?"

"I agree with you. We have to find Boyd."

"That's what I've been trying to do all day." Nick recounted his encounter with Sonny Telicky. "I was trying to figure out my next move when you called. What do you suggest?"

"Talking to Earline Barnett. If the woman with Boyd is her sister, Earline might know something."

Nick slid out of the booth and dropped a ten-dollar bill on the table. "Let's go."

Jason chugged what was left in his mug and followed him out the door. Nick snorted when he spotted the Silverado next to his car. Benny was asleep on the passenger side. Razor rolled down the window. "Back-up," was all he said.

Nick's phone sounded. When he saw Ivy's name, he laughed, turned off the phone and slipped it back in his pocket. "Follow us," he said to Razor and got in his car.

45 RAQUELLE REDUX

"C'mon," Kate waved for Ivy to follow her back to the living room. "Let's finish our gin rummy game."

"All right." Ivy looked at her watch. "But at exactly 9:15 I'm going to call Nick."

"That's really unnecessary. You saw Benny and Razor pull out of the driveway just now. They won't let anything happen to him."

"I have to admit, I was relieved when they agreed to follow him." She shook her head and smiled. "Men! They're really funny, aren't they? They bond over being in danger together."

"Oh, yeah. They don't have to say two words to each other, just fend off the enemy in one little skirmish and they're best buds."

"And apparently, when peril beckons, they don't need any sleep. I can't believe how they're ready to hit the road any time of the day or night."

Chuckling, they picked up their cards and began to play. At exactly 9:15 Ivy reached for her phone and tapped in Nick's number. After a moment she frowned and disconnected.

"All he said was he just got there, he's alive and well and hung up. He didn't let me say a word."

"I can't wait to hear what Jason has to tell him." Kate handed the cards to Ivy. "Your deal."

"Me too." Ivy shuffled the cards.

"Whatever it is, he sure doesn't want his uncle to know he's talking to Nick. Stillwell Taphouse is really off the beaten path."

After the next hand, as Kate started to shuffle the cards, the dogs began barking.

"Must be a deer in the yard," she said.

The barking grew louder and a furious knocking rattled the door.

"What now?" Kate said dropping her cards and jumping up.

Together Kate and Ivy ran to the kitchen door. Raquelle stood outside, a wild look on her face. "Oh, thank God you're here!" she said.

Kate opened the door wide. "Come in. What's wrong?"

"I got a call from Tommy. He found your friend."

"Where? Where?" Ivy waved her hands frantically.

"He said she was in a barn at that abandoned farm off of the Old Mill Road…"

"Was?" Ivy interrupted. "What do you mean was?"

Kate put her hand on Ivy's arm. "Calm down, Ivy. Let her tell us the whole story."

Ivy nodded and took a deep breath. "Sorry. Go ahead, Raquelle."

"That's just it. There's nothing else to tell. Tommy just barely got out that he found your friend. He told me where, and then the phone call got dropped. I tried redialing, but it just rings out." She grabbed hold of Kate's hand. "There isn't much gas in my car and I don't have any money. Can you drive me out to that farm?

"Of course," Kate said running to the laundry room.

"I'm going to phone Nick," Ivy called to her as she disappeared through the doorway.

She pulled out her phone and hit redial, shaking her head as Kate returned to the kitchen with a broom, a rake and the flashlight she'd used to bean Sonny Telicky's skinny sidekick.

"Oh, no! It's going to voicemail," Ivy said. "Nick, I know we promised not to leave the house, but Tommy Cranston found Holly in an abandoned barn. We're going there now. Call me as soon as you get this."

Kate put the flashlight under her arm and held out the rake to Ivy and the broom to Raquelle.

"What's this for?" Raquelle looked at Kate as if she'd lost her mind.

"Protection," Kate replied.

"What if they have guns?" Ivy asked.

Raquelle handed the broom back to Kate and reached into her jacket pocket, pulling out a small handgun. "I don't need that. Now, let's go."

46 EARLINE BARNETT

"To what do I owe this pleasure?" Earline Barnett leaned on the door jamb and smiled. She wore an oversized tee-shirt that fell off one shoulder exposing a red bra strap. Her tight-fitting denim cutoffs revealed a pair of shapely, tanned legs.

"We need to ask you some questions, Earline. Can we come in?"

"Sure, darlin'." With one hand she smoothed back her auburn hair. With the other she opened the door wide. "You know you're always welcome here, Jason. Who's your friend?" she asked as she batted her eyelashes at Nick.

"This is Detective Nick Manelli," Jason replied as the two men stepped inside.

"Oooh! Italian," Earline crooned, giving Nick the once over. "I hear they make the best lovers."

Nick stared at her stone-faced.

"This isn't a social call, Earline," Jason intervened. "We're trying to track down Boyd Leggett."

A disgusted frown replaced Earline's coquettish smile. "Why come see me?" She walked over and dropped onto the slipcovered couch. "You got the wrong sister. You should be talking to Roxy."

"Do you know where we can find her?" Jason asked.

"How should I know?" Earline reached for the pack of Virginia Slims sitting on a small folding patio table beside the couch. Lighting up, she took a puff and added, "I'm not my sister's keeper."

"She could be in trouble," Jason said. "Big trouble."

Earline eyed him a moment. "What kind of trouble?"

"Five to twenty-five years in prison for kidnapping," Nick replied.

"Kidnapping!" For the first time since they'd arrived, Earline looked alarmed. Glancing at the floor, she said. "I told her that Boyd was only gonna get her knocked up or knocked down."

Jason sat down beside her. "We know Boyd was at your grandfolks' old farmhouse with a woman he kidnapped yesterday. We also found his mother's body in the Leggett house. She was dead three months and he's been making withdrawals from her checking account all that time. We also found evidence that he's running drugs."

Earline puffed furiously as Jason spoke, but said nothing.

"If the kidnap victim dies before we find them, your sister will spend the rest of her life in prison," Nick added.

Earline snuffed out her cigarette in the ashtray, her sex kitten personae completely vanished. "I don't know where Roxy is. Last week she was here bragging about how Boyd was supposed to come into some money and how they were leaving this town for good. She didn't tell me where."

"Can you tell us the names of any friends Boyd might go to for help?" Jason asked.

Earline clicked her tongue. "Friends? That's a joke. Boyd doesn't have any friends. He owes half the town money, including me."

"They still might come to you," Nick said. "If they do, you should try to convince your sister to turn herself in."

"I can try, but she won't listen to me." Earline shook her head.

Jason stood up. "One last question. Besides the old farmhouse, do you know any other place they might go to hide out?"

Earline threw her head back and laughed. "Funny you should ask that. I told Boyd he should try drawing a map like those maps to homes of the stars in Hollywood, only his would be a map of abandoned properties in Sullivan County. For throwing parties or stashing stolen goods, he knew every one of 'em."

Jason walked to the door, where Nick was already waiting. "Like the detective said, if you hear from Roxy, you call me."

A seductive smile returned to Earline's face. "Can I call you even if I don't hear from her?"

Jason shook his head. "Goodnight, Earline."

Outside, Razor leaned on the Silverado as Benny paced back and forth. When the door opened, the big guy got in the truck while Benny ran over to Nick.

“Did you turn your phone off, man?”

Nick nodded.

“Ivy called. You’re not gonna like this.”

47 THE BARN

"Okay, slow down," Raquelle said as they drove past a sign that read "Live Bait". "The turn-off is coming up, but it's not easy to spot during the day. In the dark, we might just fly past it."

Kate looked in the rearview mirror as she reduced her speed to a crawl. "I'm grateful no one is behind us."

"Just pull over and let me out." Raquelle put her hand on the door handle. "I think I have a better shot at finding it if I'm on foot."

"Do you want me to go with you?" Ivy asked from the back seat as Kate brought the car to a complete stop.

"No, but hand me the flashlight." Raquelle grasped the light and got out of the car. She quickly disappeared into the darkness and all Kate and Ivy could see was the light beam moving down the side of the road.

"I'm scared," Ivy said wrapping her arms around herself to control her trembling.

"Me too." Kate's eyes never left the bouncing light beam. "There! She's pointing the light straight back at us. She must have found the road in."

Kate slowly drove the car forward. When she stopped, Raquelle jumped back in.

"This is it," she said. "I've only been out to this place once years ago when I was still in school. It was a dairy farm and they brought us out on a daytrip. I'm not sure, but I think it's about a half-mile to the barn."

"We should walk in, right?" Ivy asked.

"Yeah," Raquelle replied. "I could go alone."

"No way." Ivy hit redial on her phone again. "Damn! Nick's phone is still off."

"Okay, Kate," Raquelle said. "Pull in and park."

The three women exited the car. The flashlight in one hand and her gun in the other, Raquelle took the lead. They walked in silence until they finally reached a clearing. The moon provided just enough light for them to make out the barn outline. One side of the double-doors was slightly ajar.

"No vehicles around," Raquelle whispered. "And it doesn't look like there's any light on inside."

"I think I should go up to the barn alone," Ivy said.

"What? No!" Kate grabbed her arm.

"Listen to me," Ivy said. "If the kidnappers are in there, it's best if they think I'm alone." She handed her phone and the shovel to Kate. "If they drag me in there, you two can wait until Nick finally answers. If they come out, Raquelle can shoot them. Now give me the flashlight."

"I don't like this." Kate took the phone.

"She's right," Raquelle said, handing Ivy the flashlight

Ivy took a deep breath, turned and headed up the path to the barn door. She could feel her heart pounding. The flashlight beam bounced erratically as her hand shook. She stopped a few feet shy of the door and listened. Not a sound came from inside. Inching forward, she reached for the door. The old hinges squeaked as she pulled it wide open and shone the light inside.

Her eyes filled with tears and she dropped to the ground. Kate and Raquelle came running. Raquelle grabbed the flashlight and entered the barn. Kate sank beside Ivy.

"She's not here," Ivy sobbed. "She's not here."

Kate put her arm around Ivy's shoulder and held her as she wept.

Raquelle came back out of the barn. "Somebody was here. There's a snake cut in two in there and it looks like a fresh kill." She looked up at the moon and screamed, "Tommy! Where the hell are you?"

Ivy knelt forward and Kate helped her to her feet.

"Raquelle, I'm so sorry. I forgot Tommy's missing, too." She reached out and hugged the worried mother.

"Let's go," Kate said, picking up the flashlight and leading the way.

Halfway back to the car, they froze as they spotted headlights coming their way. Raquelle pulled out her handgun and aimed, but the vehicle came to a complete stop.

"Ivy! Kate!" a male voiced called out.

"Yeah, it's us," Ivy shouted back.

"You can lower your gun, Raquelle," Kate said. "The cavalry has arrived."

The three women walked toward the headlights as Nick jogged towards them, Jason, Razor and Benny behind him.

"What did I tell you?" He glared at Ivy. "You're worse than your sister."

Ivy said nothing as she walked over, stopping just a few inches in front of Nick. The others watched and Benny gasped audibly as she slapped Nick's chest with her open hands. "And what about you?" She pointed a finger at him. "If you had left your phone on, I would have been able to talk to you. But no! No, Mr. Macho Man, nobody's supposed to check up on you or worry about you, right?"

She started to walk away, then turned back, now poking her finger in his chest. "Do you honestly think I could sit home playing gin rummy after Raquelle told us her son found Holly? Do you?"

Nick lowered his head as Ivy lifted hers and stamped off in the direction of the car.

"And what the hell are you doin' here, Bascom?" Raquelle sneered. "Looking for Tommy so you could run back to your uncle and get a pat on the head?"

Jason said nothing as Raquelle spit on the ground in his direction, then took off after Ivy.

Kate looked at Jason. "My Italian grandmother couldn't have done that better." As she walked past Nick she said, "I now know why Holly broke up with you." She followed Raquelle, dragging the shovel and broom behind her.

48 THE HEN HOUSE

Nick stood quietly for a minute, then turned to Razor. "Could you drive the truck up to the door so we can have a look inside?"

Razor nodded and jogged back to the Silverado. Nick, Jason and Benny walked up to the barn and pulled both doors open. Razor stopped the truck just inside the entrance and flipped on the high-beams.

Inside the barn, Nick walked over to where the snake lay, split in two, the shovel on the floor beside it.

Holly hates snakes.

As he surveyed the rest of the barn, his eyes came to rest on the rusted metal wheel. Kneeling down he examined the broken spoke. When he stood back up and looked across the floor, he spotted the hammer.

Jason came up behind him. "Think somebody used the hammer to break the spoke?"

"Yep," Nick replied. "There were cuff marks on the bedpost at the farmhouse. If they cuffed her to that wheel, maybe this Tommy Cranston used the hammer to get her loose."

"Wow," Benny said. "Amazing how you put two and four together like that."

"Two and two, Benny," Razor said softly.

"It's possible they got away." Jason looked to the door. "I can call the canine unit from Monticello tomorrow. They have dogs that track. I'll come out and dust for fingerprints, too."

Nick nodded, looking across the barn one more time.

Hang in there, Holly. We're getting close.

"Let's go," he said. "We can't do anything more tonight.

Nick and Jason climbed in the crew cab, Benny and Razor in front.

When they got back on paved road, Benny chuckled. "Hey, Nick. Kate and Ivy were pretty steamed at you. You want to bunk with us tonight, seeing as how you're in the hen house."

"Dog house," Benny said, shaking his head.

"Kate doesn't have a doghouse," Benny replied.

****

Encouraged that the back light was left on, Nick slowly mounted the porch steps. Relieved when the door knob turned in his hand, he gave Benny and Razor a wave and stepped inside Kate's kitchen. A small light over the stove gave the room a warm glow. He opened the refrigerator and felt a lump form in his throat at the sight of twelve cans of Michelob

Ultra -- Holly's favorite. He grabbed one, popped the tab and sank on a chair at the breakfast counter.

As he took a swallow of the beer, he felt a paw on his leg. Lucky sat in front of him, a mournful look on her face.

"Yeah, I miss her, too," he said, patting the dog on the head. He downed the rest of the beer, dropped the can in the trash and tiptoed upstairs. Kate's and Ivy's doors were shut. Benny was right. They were plenty steamed at him. Ivy was right, too. He should not have turned off his phone.

Kate's comment hurt most of all. He felt certain Holly had broken up with him because she had cold feet, never having been married before. But was it his fault? Had he been too -- too what? Bossy? Macho?

In the bathroom, he stared at himself in the mirror. *I can work on that. Just please let me find her.*

When he opened the door, Lucky sat waiting for him. She followed him into the bedroom and as he got into bed, she hopped up beside him.

"Looks like you're the only one not mad at me tonight."

She licked his face, lay down and rested her head on his stomach. Putting his hand on the dog's back, he said, "Tomorrow. Tomorrow we're going to find her."

49 THE NOSE KNOWS

Nick opened his eyes and looked at the clock. 6:30. As soon as he sat up, Lucky jumped off the bed. Dressing quickly, Nick opened the bedroom door. Kate and Ivy's doors were still shut.

In the kitchen, he found Lucky's leash and attached it to her collar. As he went to the door, Amy and Winston appeared.

"Uh-uh. You two, stay. I'm not taking all three of you." Nick opened the door and guided Lucky out.

As they walked down the driveway, he said, "Let's go downtown and get some doughnuts for Kate and Ivy. That might soften them up a little bit."

When they got near the bottom of the hill, Lucky pulled on the leash to go up a side road.

"No, Lucky. This way." Nick tugged on the leash, but the dog resisted. "C'mon."

Nick tried to coax her, but the dog wouldn't budge and just turned her head to look up the side road. When she began to whimper, Nick stared at the dog. He'd never seen her behave like this. Suddenly, he wondered what was at the top of that hill.

"Okay, Lucky. Let's go," he said, picking up his pace as the dog started to trot. Once they passed the house on the corner, there was nothing but woods on the left side of the street. The right side sloped downward to another house, but once they passed that yard, nothing but trees lined both sides of the road. Lucky strained at the leash. Nick broke into a full run behind the dog.

He felt a blast of adrenaline when a run-down house came into view as they reached the top of the hill. He stopped, remembering he was unarmed. Lucky looked at him then at the house. She tugged at the leash and began a gentle whine that escalated into a full bark.

Any chance of sneaking up to the house evaporated. Nick released Lucky from the leash and she raced to the back of the house, whimpering as she frantically clawed at the door. Nick followed and peered in the back window.

Holly!

Inside, she was sitting on the floor, cuffed to a radiator, her eyes closed. "Holly," he called, but she didn't stir.

Please be alive.

When the doorknob wouldn't turn, without hesitation, he kicked it in. Lucky rushed past him and ran to Holly, nudging her arm with her nose, whimpering as her tail wagged wildly. After a moment, Holly opened her eyes. "Lucky," was all she said, looking up as Nick knelt beside her.

"Am I having that dream again?" she asked blinking. Nick put both hands on either side of her face and kissed her.

“This time it feels real,” she said, closing her eyes, appearing unable to stay awake. Nick felt her pulse.

Standing up, he pulled out his phone and hit speed dial, relieved when Kate answered on the first ring. “Kate. I found Holly in the abandoned house -- the one on top of the hill. Yeah, the last left turn before you reach the bottom of your road. Call 911 and get an ambulance here. She can’t seem to stay awake and her pulse is weak. She may be dehydrated or drugged. Then call the sheriff. Hurry.”

He got back down on the floor and examined the spot where the cuffs were attached to the leg of the radiator. The floor under the radiator was warped. If he could find a lever, he could probably lift the radiator. He got back up and scanned the room for something he could use. In the corner he spotted a mop, the old-fashioned kind, solid-wood. He grabbed the handle and walked back over to the radiator.

“Lucky, you got to move.” The dog lay with her paw on Holly’s leg, her back end blocking the spot he needed to position the mop handle. She stared at Holly’s face, paying no attention to Nick.

“Believe me, I understand,” he said as he bent down and gently slid the dog out of the way. He positioned the top end of the mop handle in a crack in the floor beneath the radiator. One push and the floor board split as the radiator foot rose up. Holly’s eyes opened as the cuff dropped to the floor.

“Holly -- honey, move your arm.”

She looked at him blankly, unmoving. He nudged her arm forward with his foot, then lowered the radiator. Reaching down he helped her to her feet, then picked her up and carried her outside. He sat down on the edge of the dilapidated porch floor with Holly in his lap and hugged her to him. Lucky sat down in front of them, watching.

After a time, Holly lifted her head from his shoulder and stared. “Nick, is it really you?”

“Yeah,” he smiled. “It’s really me.”

“I thought I was never going to see you again,” she said running her uncuffed hand down his cheek. “I’ve been so wrong…”

“Maybe I’ve been wrong about a few things, too,” he said.

“Nick, will you marry me?” she asked.

“In a heartbeat,” he answered.

“Okay. Name the date,” she said as she dropped her head back on his shoulder, a smile on her face.

50 REHYDRATION

Ivy reached over the sidebar of the hospital bed and squeezed Holly's hand. Holly opened her eyes.

"You can relax." Holly smiled, squeezing back. "Now stop waking me up."

"Sorry, but I can't help myself. You had us so scared."

Holly tried stretching her hands over her head, but the IV restricted her movement. "Can't wait until I'm in a bed where I'm not tied to something," she laughed.

Both sisters looked to the door as Kate breezed in with a cardboard box in her hand. Three paper coffee cups anchored the corners and a bag sat propped in the middle. "How we doing?" she asked as she put the box on the rolling table at the foot of the bed.

"Did you get it?" Holly sat up, an anxious look on her face.

Kate opened the bag, extracting a giant, glazed bear claw. "As you requested."

"You look like a kid in a candy store," Ivy giggled as Holly reached for the bear claw and bit into it.

"Mmm," she moaned, closing her eyes. When she re-opened them, her expression turned serious. "It's amazing the things you crave when you're afraid you'll never have them again."

"I hope Nick Manelli was one of those things," Ivy said, her face turning stern. "Now that you're nearly rehydrated and you're eating, we need to talk. You had a lot of nerve letting us think he broke up with you."

"Yeah," Kate said. "I admit -- he's an Italian man and he can be a little high-handed, but he didn't even hesitate when Ivy called him and told him you'd been kidnapped. He got right in the car, and we had to give him directions by phone as he drove."

"And I don't think he slept since he got here. He loves you, Holly. You tell him you're going to marry him, or -- or -- I don't know, but I'll think of some way to make you miserable."

Holly said nothing as she continued to devour the bear claw, bits of glaze on her cheeks and down the front of her hospital gown. As she took a sip of coffee, Nick walked in the room.

"Speak of the devil," Kate laughed. She and Ivy giggled as he walked straight over to the bed and gave Holly what the three of them used to call a "soap opera kiss".

"Delicious." He licked his lips and brushed glaze crumbs off her face. Without taking his eyes off the patient, he asked, "Did Holly tell you she asked me to marry her?"

"No!" Ivy and Kate squealed simultaneously.

"Yeah, she even told me to name the date."

"Holly, I can't believe you let us go on and on and all the while you two had made up." Ivy shook her head, grinning.

Gazing into Nick's eyes, Holly held out the bear claw and he took a bite.

"Aw, c'mon, Ivy," Kate said, tapping her on the arm and heading to the door. "We're going to get diabetes watching them." She reached for the door handle and stopped. "Nick, what I said last night -- forget it."

"You said something to me last night?" Nick asked, his eyes fixed on Holly.

Kate just smiled and laced her arm through Ivy's. As she was being pulled out the door, Ivy said, "I don't know if you're listening, but I'm really happy for you both."

Holly sighed. "Kate told me you got right in the car when they called to tell you I was missing."

Nick took her hand and kissed her palm. "What else would I do?"

"Oh, I don't know. How about telling them I wasn't your problem anymore?"

"Did you honestly think that I was going to let you go just because you called off the wedding?"

"Well, yeah. I mean, I basically broke up with you and you did let me go."

"I knew you just had cold feet. I was giving you time. That's all."

"Really?"

"Really." Caressing her neck with his right hand, he kissed her again. "I was just waiting for Ivy's visit. I knew she'd talk some sense into you."

She slapped his shoulder half-heartedly. “You were that sure of yourself?”

“Of course. When you called off the wedding, you talked some nonsense about being incompatible, and you needed your space and yada yada yada. But there were three things you didn’t say.”

Holly’s eyes became slits. “And what were those three things?”

“You didn’t say ‘I don’t love you anymore’. You didn’t say ‘I found someone else’. And you didn’t say ‘I never want to see you again’.”

“I love you Nick Manelli.

“I love you more, Holly Manelli nee Donnelly.”

“About that name change thing…”

Nick pulled back and stared at her. After a moment, he said, “Okay, we can talk about that.”

Pulling him close, Holly covered his mouth with hers.

51 HOME SWEET HOME

"This is heaven," Holly said as she nestled into the chaise cushions on Kate's front porch.

Ivy smiled, placing a lunch tray on her sister's lap. "A BLT with extra mayo, just like you ordered."

Holly grinned as she picked up half the sandwich and admired it. After a moment she took a bite and moaned in delight. "Oh, so good."

"Don't get too used to this," Kate said as she walked out onto the porch and handed Holly a mug.

"I know, I know," Holly laughed. "You'll indulge me for a day or two, but after that you two will be back to abusing me. What's this?" she asked as she sniffed the steaming liquid in the mug.

"It's chamomile tea," Kate replied. "It helps with rehydration."

"I'd rather a Michelob Ultra," Holly chuckled, taking a sip. "But this isn't bad. You know, when I asked Tommy if I could have died from a bite from the snake he killed, he assured me you probably had something in the yard that could heal me."

"Holly!" a shout interrupted from across the yard. Benny jogged over as Razor followed at his more measured pace. Bounding up the steps, Benny bent over and gave her a hug. "We almost thought we were never going to see you again."

"For quite a while, I thought that, too."

"Welcome home," Razor said as he walked over and tapped the toe of her shoe.

"Thanks, Razor. And thank you both. Kate and Ivy filled me in on all you did to help find me."

"No problem," Benny said. "You just illiterate the whole episode from your memory."

"Eliminate." Razor scratched his neck.

"Hey, so you and Nick back together?" Benny asked. "That guy's got it bad for you…"

"Benny," Razor made eye contact with his friend and shook his head.

"It's alright, Razor," Holly laughed. "Nick and I are back together."

The big man's usually somber face transformed into a smile and Benny patted Holly's shoulder. "That's great. You should have the wedding right here in Kate's yard."

Kate nodded. "The flower beds have never looked lovelier."

"Could you all just relax please. There's no rush here." Holly took another bite of her sandwich.

"Nick said you told him to name the date." Ivy waggled her head. "I'm not so sure he wouldn't want to get married sooner rather than later."

"Yeah." Kate stood beside Ivy and imitated Ivy's head waggle. "Before you change your mind again."

Holly glared at the pair, then took another huge bite out of her sandwich.

"Where is Nick?" Benny asked.

"He went downtown to give a statement to the sheriff," Kate replied.

Benny turned to Razor. "Maybe we ought to go down and make sure he doesn't do anything crazy."

Holly covered her mouth with her hand to conceal an amused smile as she pictured Benny counseling Nick. When she finally managed to swallow, she chuckled. "I wouldn't worry about Nick. He knows how to handle guys like Bascom."

"Oh, I don't know about that." Benny shook his head. "The last time we waited for him outside the sheriff's office, Razor here actually got worried 'cause Nick got right up in Bascom's face."

"That was before he found Holly." Ivy smiled politely. "I'm sure he's much more in control of his feelings now. In fact, that's probably him." She lifted her chin in the direction of the driveway.

Everyone turned at the sound of a car engine coming up the road.

As a red Honda pulled into the driveway, Holly asked, "Who's that?"

"Raquelle." Kate answered frowning. "I should have called her to let her know we found you. I wonder if she's heard from Tommy."

"Oh, gosh." Holly put her plate down on the side table. "You know he saved my life. I forgot he's still missing."

Raquelle got out of the car and ran over to the porch. Her eyes were red and her hair disheveled.

"Tommy's been arrested."

52 ARREST

"Any leads on Boyd Leggett?" Nick asked as he handed Jason Bascom his signed statement.

The deputy just shook his head looking down at the document in his hand. "There's an APB out on him, but nothing yet."

"I have a lot of vacation time coming to me." Nick waited for Jason to make eye contact. When he didn't look up, Nick continued. "I'd be happy to help search abandoned properties with you."

Jason's eyes remained fixed on the report when the front door of the police station opened.

"Get in there, you worthless slimeball." Cyrus Bascom pushed a handcuffed Tommy Cranston into the station. Tommy had a split lip and what looked like the start of a black eye. The sheriff scowled when he spotted Nick. Grabbing Tommy's shoulder, he pushed him towards Jason's desk.

"Jason, lock up this cockweasel. He's under arrest for the murder of Chuck Dwyer. Charges include resisting a police officer."

Tommy sighed. "I didn't resist anything, unless asking a question..."

Bascom shoved Tommy past the chair where Nick sat, knocking the boy to the floor. Nick stood up and turned, providing a partial block between the sheriff and the fallen boy. Jason jumped up from his chair and helped Tommy to his feet.

"Excuse me, Sheriff," Nick said as the deputy disappeared with Tommy through a door behind the sheriff's desk. "I just provided Officer Bascom with my statement about Holly Donnelly's kidnapping, and I want you to know I volunteered my services to assist in the search for Boyd Leggett."

Bascom glared at Nick for a moment. The glare slowly morphed into an insincere smile. "Well, Detective, we thank you for that kind offer, but at this time we don't need your services."

"Really?" Nick returned the smile. "Seems you have an awful lot on your plate for a two-man department."

The sheriff's eyes became slits. "Well, I'll keep your offer in mind."

The front door opened again and the sheriff turned around. Mary Harris bustled over to her desk. "Sorry, I'm so late, Sheriff," she said, dropping her bag on her desk and turning on her computer.

Bascom grunted and turned back to Nick. "As I said, Detective, right now we can handle our workload just fine. Thank you for coming in." He walked over to his desk and sat down.

Nick headed to the front door when the phone rang.

"Reddington Manor Police Department," Mary said. "Just a moment." She pressed the hold button. "Sheriff, it's Judge Maddox for you."

As Bascom picked up the phone and swiveled his chair to face the back wall, Jason returned to his desk. Nick gave him a wave and left the office. Jason glanced over at Bascom who appeared engrossed in his phone conversation. Reaching for a pen and Nick's statement, he walked to the door. Nick had his hand on the car door handle as Jason stepped outside.

"Pretend you're signing this," Jason said.

Nick took the pen and faked his signature. With his eyes on the paper, he asked, "Something you want to say to me, Officer?"

Jason bit his lip. "Look for an email from me."

Nick looked up and smiled, handing Jason the paper and pen. "Do you think the boy in there killed Chuck Dwyer?"

Jason lowered his eyes. "I -- I don't know."

"Do you think Boyd Leggett killed him?"

Jason didn't answer.

Nick put his hands on the car roof and widened his smile. "Deputy, it's clear to me your uncle doesn't want Boyd Leggett found. Just so you know, I'm going to find him and I'm going to find out why."

Jason made eye contact with Nick for the first time that morning. "Just look for an email from me."

53 A LOT TO ASK

Kate ran down the porch steps and put her arm around Raquelle. As the woman's knees buckled, Razor moved quickly to help get her on the porch. Practically carrying her up the steps, he guided her onto one of the wicker chairs. Ivy ran inside and returned with a box of tissues.

Kate knelt beside Raquelle and took her hand. "Tell us what happened."

Raquelle reached for a tissue and wiped the tears from her eyes. "I don't really know. I just got a call from Tommy. He said the sheriff arrested him for killing Chuck."

"Oh, no," Kate sighed.

"That's messed up," Benny said. "Of all people, Tommy would never kill Chuck. Tommy wouldn't kill anybody."

"Tell that to that animal, Cyrus Bascom," Raquelle said, blowing her nose.

Holly sat forward. "Tommy saved my life. I'll do anything I can to help you. Do you have a lawyer?"

The distressed mother shook her head.

"Okay, that's the first thing we need to do." Holly looked at Kate.

"I don't really know any lawyers, except for the local guy who does wills and closings." Kate grimaced.

"We can maybe help you with some names, right, Razor?" Benny said.

Holly smiled. "Great."

"We need to wait for Nick before we do anything," Ivy said.

"Oh, yeah," Holly tapped the side of her head with her palm. "What am I thinking? Raquelle, my -- my fiancé, Nick is a detective. He's down at the station right now. He'll know exactly what we should do."

Benny looked to Razor who just nodded. "Okay, you ladies wait here," Benny said. "We're gonna go downtown and get Nick."

"Good," Kate said. As the two men crossed the yard, she asked, "Have you eaten anything this morning, Raquelle?"

When the woman shook her head, Kate stood up. "Let me go make lunch for everyone."

"I'll help." Ivy started to follow Kate inside.

"I hear a car," Holly said standing up.

Razor and Benny had just reached the Silverado, when Nick's car appeared. Holly was already in the driveway by the time he came to a stop behind the red Honda.

"What are you doing up?" Nick asked as he got out of the car and put his arm around Holly's waist.

"Hey, man, Everything okay?" Benny asked as he and Razor walked over to where the couple stood.

Nick nodded. "Yeah." He looked to the porch. "What's going on?"

"Could you guys give us a minute?" Holly asked.

Razor nodded and pulled Benny back to the porch before he could answer.

Holly rested her forehead on Nick's chest, then leaned back and looked up at him. "Look I know this is a lot to ask, but…"

"You want me to help find Chuck's murderer."

"How could you know that?" she asked, appearing bewildered.

"Bascom brought a teenager into the station while I was there. Said he arrested him for the murder of Chuck Dwyer."

"That was Tommy Cranston."

"The kid who killed the snake?"

Holly nodded. "His mother, Raquelle, is the woman on the porch."

Nick looked over Holly's head to where Raquelle sat.

"You'll help her, won't you?"

Nick looked into her eyes and smiled. "For you -- anything."

She returned her forehead to his chest and squeezed him tightly. "What was that?" she said, leaning back.

He chuckled as he reached in his back pocket and pulled out his vibrating phone. He glanced at the screen and saw the email from Jason had arrived.

"Anything important?" she asked.

He moved his arm from her waist to her shoulder and started toward the porch. “Could be,” was all he said.

54 A PLAN

As Kate and Ivy served lunch to everyone in the kitchen, Nick walked into the living room and looked at his cellphone. He opened the email Jason sent him and clicked on the attachment. A list of abandoned properties in Sullivan County filled the screen.

Jason clearly didn't want his uncle to know he was sharing this list with him. Or was that an act? Was this list just something to occupy him and keep him off track? It seemed that Boyd Leggett was always one step ahead of them. Was someone keeping him informed of where they would be looking next? Was it Cyrus? Or, was it Jason?

Still, Jason had taken him to talk to the Barnett woman and then gone with them to the abandoned barn. And he did check for fingerprints at the Barnett's farmhouse even though his uncle balked at Nick's suggestion.

Nick didn't like being in this position. A lack of cooperation from local law enforcement made the job of investigating a crime difficult -- especially when he couldn't be sure he could completely trust the one insider who appeared to be trying to help him.

It didn't matter. He had no doubt it was Boyd Leggett who kidnapped Holly, and for that he was going to pay. But did he kill Chuck Dwyer? Nick wasn't so sure about that. If not Boyd, who? Tommy Cranston? Nick doubted that.

He tapped the screen for recent calls, then hit Jason's number.

"Got the email," he said when the deputy answered. After a silent pause, he said. "I need another favor."

****

"Anyone want more iced tea?" Kate held up the pitcher.

"I do." Benny handed her his glass.

Nick walked into the room and everyone turned their eyes to him. "Okay. Here's the plan," he said. "Razor, I texted you a list of abandoned properties in Sullivan County. I'd like you and Benny to start searching the nearest ones. If you think you found Boyd Leggett, you call me and wait until I get there. Do not make contact. Is that understood?"

Benny raised his hand as if in school. "But what if we find the peep and he starts to leave?"

"Perp," Razor said as he pulled out his cellphone.

"Follow at a safe distance," Nick replied.

"Aw." Benny frowned. "You're not gonna let us take at least one swing at him? I mean, he deserves a beating just for what he did to his mother -- not to mention what he did to Holly."

"You leave him to me," Nick replied.

"Oh, I get it," Benny guffawed as he poked Razor in the ribs. Under his breath, he said, "I'd pay money to see that."

"Jason Bascom said that the sheriff will be out of the office from noon to two," Nick continued. "Ivy, Raquelle, you and I will go down to the sheriff's office and talk to Tommy."

"Why Ivy? Why not me?" Kate sat up straight, placing her fists on the table.

"Because, on the chance the sheriff returns to the office while we're there, Ivy's got a better history with Bascom than you." Nick pierced her with his laser beam stare.

Kate grunted and sank back in her chair.

"Holly, I want you to call Yolanda and tell her to find out whatever she can on Boyd Leggett and Cyrus Bascom. Also, tell her to let Tony Fratelli, the bail bondsman, know I'm going to need that favor he owes me."

Holly just smiled.

"Oh, so I've got nothing to do?" Kate crossed her arms in front of her.

"You stay by the phone. Benny, you call Kate and keep her informed of where you are and where you're headed."

"Boring," Kate sighed.

Nick scowled at her. "You also need to stay here with Holly. She's in no condition to do anything more than make a phone call, and I don't want anyone left alone."

Holly made eye contact with Kate, raising one eyebrow. Kate's expression softened.

Nick exhaled audibly as he scanned the table. All eyes were on him. "Look, a man's been murdered and Holly was held hostage and left for dead. This isn't a game we're playing. I want to catch whoever is responsible, but it's more important to me that none of you gets hurt in the process. No one is to go anywhere alone. Is that clear?"

Everyone nodded, including Kate.

55 THE WHOLE TRUTH

Nick held the door to the police station open for Raquelle and Ivy. Inside he looked past Mary Harris's empty desk to the back of the office where Jason sat. The deputy stood up and walked over to the door he had lead Tommy Cranston through earlier in the day.

"Raquelle…" he said as she neared him.

"Just shut up and open the door, Jason," she spat.

He paused, appearing to want to say more, then just lowered his eyes and put the key in the lock. Raquelle and Ivy stepped through the doorway. Before following them, Nick stopped.

"I appreciate this," he said.

"Just don't take too long." Jason walked back to his desk.

When Nick walked through the doorway, Raquelle was crying as she hugged Tommy the best she could through the cell bars. Ivy just stood watching, her eyes glistening.

"Tommy, I'm Nick Manelli. I'm a detective from New Jersey. I need to ask you some questions, and we don't have a lot of time."

Tommy nodded.

"Where were you the night Chuck Dwyer was murdered?"

"He was home with me," Raquelle's eyes blazed as she released Tommy and turned on Nick.

"Mom, you know that's not true." Tommy looked up at Nick. "I was at a bar with my friends."

"Why did you run away if you have an alibi?" Nick asked.

"The friends I was with all have juvenile records. Bascom is always out to get them. If they had to testify, he'd find some reason to arrest them."

"What about the bartender?" Nick asked. When Tommy hesitated, Nick sighed. "How old are you?"

"Seventeen."

"So this bar you go to serves minors and the bartender will deny you and your friends were ever there."

Again, Tommy just nodded.

"When you talked to Kate, you said there was more going on than Chuck's murder. What did you mean?"

As Tommy frowned, Nick moved closer. "Look, son. If you want my help, you need to tell me the whole truth, no matter what."

Tommy took a deep breath. "Okay. I knew Boyd was selling drugs, and I figured he was keeping them in the house. The night before Chuck died, I sneaked into the Leggett house looking for weed."

"Tommy!" Raquelle slapped at the bars and Tommy stepped back.

"Sorry, Mom," he said. Turning back to Nick, he continued. "When I found Mrs. Leggett upstairs, I ran out of there as fast as I could. Unfortunately, Boyd was pulling into the driveway when I got outside."

"He saw you come out of the house?"

"I don't think so, but I'm not sure. He saw me in the yard though. He swore at me -- said he'd get Bascom after me. When I said there were a few things about him that I could tell Bascom, he just laughed. Said he had more on Bascom, than Bascom had on him."

Nick sighed and scratched the back of his neck. "All right. I'm going to need the name of the bar and the names of your friends and the bartender."

Tommy lowered his head.

"Tommy, you tell him the names." Raquelle said putting her hands on the cell bars.

"I can't." Tommy's face reflected pure anguish.

"You tell him the names, right now. Was it Hank? Tory?"

Tommy just shook his head.

"Tell him!" Raquelle shouted through the cell bars. Ivy put her hand on her shoulder.

"Okay, Tommy," Nick intervened. "You don't have to tell me anything right now. I'll be back tomorrow. That should give you enough time to think about spending the rest of your life in a cage like this one."

"That's right, Tommy," Raquelle said in a calmer voice. "You go ahead and save your low-life friends from some charges that could just put them in a juvenile detention center while you spend the rest of your life in prison for murder -- for something you didn't do."

Tommy backed up and sat down on the cot, looking at the floor.

"Let's go," Nick said, looking at Ivy and tapping on the exit door.

Ivy laced her arm through Raquelle's. "C'mon," she whispered. "We can come back tomorrow."

Raquelle resisted Ivy's pull as she stared at Tommy. After a moment she shook her head and allowed Ivy to lead her past Nick out into the office.

Nick kept his eyes on Jason as the deputy watched Raquelle walk by him and out the door, a helpless look on his face. When she and Ivy were outside, Nick asked, "Do you have any hard evidence against this boy?"

"Fingerprints at Chuck Dwyer's house."

"But not on the murder weapon?"

Jason shook his head. "We also found his prints inside the Leggett house."

"But there was no crime committed there. The woman died of natural causes and no theft was ever reported, right?"

"Right." Jason looked at his watch.

"I owe you one." Nick turned and walked out the door. When he got in the car, Raquelle glared at him from the passenger seat as Ivy sat quietly in back.

"That's it? We're just going to leave him there?" she asked.

"For the time being," Nick replied putting the key in the ignition. "Do you know where to find this Hank or Tory?"

Raquelle pulled the seatbelt across her chest and jammed the metal end in the clasp. “Make a right at the light,” she snapped.

56 GLADIOLAS

Kate snapped on her fanny pack, putting in a 10-ounce bottle of water and a small pair of garden snippers. Donning her straw hat, she said, "I'll be outside."

"Wait, I'll come with you." Holly stood up and started to follow her.

"You're supposed to be resting." Kate's annoyed expression had returned.

"Oh, c'mon. You're not still mad because you have to babysit me, are you?"

Before Kate could reply, the phone rang. She walked over and lifted the hand receiver from the wall phone. "Hello -- okay -- bye."

She walked back to the counter. "That was Benny," she said, making a notation on her copy of the abandoned properties list. "That's another reason you should stay inside. Somebody needs to answer the phone."

"I'll take the cordless extension from upstairs."

Kate frowned. "Suit yourself."

Holly ran upstairs to retrieve the phone from Kate's bedroom. By the time she got outside, Kate was nowhere in sight and Flo's Kia was pulling into the driveway. Holly walked over as Flo opened the door.

"Well, I see you're still alive," Flo snorted as she turned in the car seat and placed her feet on the ground.

"Yeah," Holly smiled and nodded.

"I been waiting to see how things turned out," the big woman chuckled. "Thought maybe Kate and I could work out a deal with the funeral director -- like a twofer."

Uncertain how to reply, Holly felt the smile fading from her face as Flo got out of the car.

"I hope that means I can get that worthless nephew of mine back to work around here. I don't see the truck." Flo looked around to the back. "Where the hell is he now?"

"Well," Holly hesitated, unsure how much she should reveal to this unpleasant woman. "I'm not really sure," she finally answered.

Flo fished her cellphone out of her handbag and tapped the screen. "Damn him," she said, a disgusted frown on her face. "I'll bet he's shacked up somewhere and just not answering my call."

As Flo dropped her cellphone back in her bag, the cordless phone in Holly's hand rang. She answered.

"Kate, it's me, Benny."

Holly gave Flo a lame smile, "You'll have to excuse me." As she headed back to the porch, Flo barked after her. "You see Benny, tell him I'm looking for him."

Holly turned slightly and nodded as Flo got in the car and backed out of the driveway.

"It's Holly, not Kate, Benny. Did you hear that?"

"Yeah, I heard. Don't worry. I can handle Aunt Flo. Anyway just want you to know we're going up Peck's Hill to the next place on the list. Razor says there probably won't be any cell service up there."

"Just do like Nick said, okay?"

"Okay. Catch you later."

Holly hit the off button and scanned the yard, but Kate was still out of sight. She walked around back and spotted the top of Kate's straw hat bobbing just above the picket fence surrounding the vegetable garden.

"Here you are," she said. "Flo's here looking for Benny, but I didn't tell her anything. Then he called and said they're on their way to Peck's Hill."

Kate just grunted in reply.

Grasping the top pickets of the fence, Holly leaned over to see what Kate was doing. "Can I help?" she asked.

"No." Head down, Kate dug furiously in the ground, lifted a clump of weeds and tossed it over the fence.

Holly just shook her head and looked across into the Leggett yard. "Oh, wow. Look at those gladiolas in bloom over there."

Kate stopped digging, stood up and looked in the direction Holly pointed. "Yeah," she sighed, her expression softening. "They were Milly's favorites."

"Why don't we go over and cut them? They'd make a beautiful bouquet for the house."

Kate nodded. “You’re right. I’m sure Milly wouldn’t mind.” She opened the garden gate and stepped out of the vegetable bed. “As a matter of fact, I think she’d be happy her prize flowers would be admired and not just left in a weed patch.”

Holly smiled and followed as Kate walked to the front of the house. “I’m going to leave the phone on the step here. Benny said they probably won’t have cell service where they’re going next.”

“Yeah,” Kate agreed. “We’ll be back before they call again anyway.”

As they walked up the Leggett driveway, Kate said, “Poor Milly hasn’t even had a wake. Chuck either. With everything that’s happened, I haven’t had a chance to talk to Flo about it.”

Deciding not to tell Kate Flo’s two-fer comment, Holly said, “There’s no reason we can’t have our own wake for them. You know, tonight, when everyone’s back here. We can just have a toast and you can maybe say something about them.”

“You’re right.” Kate nodded. “There’s no reason we can’t do that. And those gladiolas will make the perfect centerpiece for the table.”

When they reached the gladiola patch, Kate unzipped her fanny pack, pulled out her garden snippers and waded through the tall grass. One by one she cut the stalks of the stately flowers and handed them to Holly.

“These are gorgeous,” Holly said, gazing at the flowers in her arms, “especially the pink tipped…”

Suddenly she was down on her butt among the weeds, Kate’s hand over her mouth. Kate placed her index finger across her own mouth, then pointed toward the back yard. The two women watched silently as a swarthy looking man scurried across the yard and into the back door of the house.

Kate whispered, “That’s Boyd.”

57 CLICK

"We've got to get out of here," Holly whispered back. Gently she lay the flowers down on the ground and got up on her knees.

"On the count of three, let's run for it," Kate said.

Holly nodded. Before Kate could start the count, the sound of hammering coming from the upstairs window caused them both to look up.

"Good," Kate said. "We don't need to run and risk making noise." She took Holly's arm and they moved quickly from the weed patch across the rutted driveway to the side of the house, directly under the open window. "Okay, now let's just walk slowly down the driveway out to the road," she whispered.

"I hear a car," Holly said softly.

"Nick, I bet." Kate started to creep forward slowly, looking out to the road. Gasping, she scurried back. "It's a police cruiser. C'mon."

Just as they reached the back porch, they could hear the car pulling into the driveway. "We have no choice," Kate said, pulling Holly by the arm up onto the porch. The back door had been left ajar. Together they tiptoed inside. Keeping her hold on

Holly's arm, Kate led her to a small latched door in the corner. She lifted the latch and put her hand on Holly's back, guiding her downward into the small pantry. Crouching, she followed and pulled the door shut.

"Who's there?" a shout came from upstairs.

Holly and Kate sat on the pantry floor as still as possible. Holly had to tilt her head a bit because the slanted ceiling of the small space consisted of the staircase bottom, reminding her of Harry Potter's bedroom under the stairs of 4 Privet Drive. What she wouldn't give for a magic wand right now.

Suddenly footsteps pounded down the stairs overhead and the two women squeezed their eyes shut as dust motes fell on them like snowflakes. At the same time, they heard the back door open.

"Oh. It's you," Boyd said as he entered the kitchen.

"Where is it?" Cyrus Bascom's voice was unmistakable.

"I'm having trouble getting the floorboard up. I thought I heard something down here. Come upstairs and help me."

The steps squeaked overhead as the two men mounted the stairs.

"Shall we make a run for it?" Kate whispered.

Holly shook her head. "I think we're safer if we wait until they go."

Kate nodded as the hammering resumed. After a few short bangs, the stairs squeaked overhead again. As the men reached the bottom of the steps, the pantry door popped open a sliver. Holly grasped Kate's wrist as she reached to pull it shut, fearing the slightest noise might give them away. Kate made eye contact and nodded slightly.

"Okay, Boyd, you can stop there," the sheriff said, his voice coming from the living room.

"What's the gun for Cyrus?" Boyd asked, sounding alarmed.

Holly and Kate gave each other wide-eyed stares.

"What do you think, you dumb cockweasel?" Cyrus snorted.

"You'll never get away with this," Boyd said.

"I already have," Cyrus chuckled. "Now just put the goods in the bag there."

Kate scanned the pantry, her eyes coming to rest on a small, whisk broom. "We have to do something," she whispered, handing Holly the broom. "In his back, this'll feel like a gun."

Before Holly could react, Kate pushed the pantry door open. Miraculously, it didn't squeak.

"How can you do this to me, Cyrus? After all I done for you."

Kate crawled out and stood up. She turned and helped Holly to her feet. As Holly watched her friend carefully unlatch her fanny pack, she realized the plan. Kate made eye contact and Holly nodded. Together they slowly crept to the living room doorway.

"What you done for me! Why you ain't never done anything for anybody but yourself in your whole life, boy," Cyrus said scornfully.

"Come on, Cyrus," Boyd whined. "Just give me enough to get out of town. There's more than enough. I swear I'll never tell anybody anything and I'll never come back."

"Oh, you're right about one thing. You'll never tell anybody anything. Now shut up and just finish loading that bag."

In the moment of silence, Holly looked at Kate, then lowered her head once in assent. Kate joined the two ends of the fanny pack straps. As soon as the connections clicked, Holly rushed into the living room, and stuck the broom handle in the sheriff's back.

"That was the sound of a cocked 45 magnum now pointed at your liver. Drop the gun, Sheriff," Holly commanded.

Before he could even respond, Kate came alongside him and reached across his chest for the pistol in his hand.

"I'll take that, Sheriff," she said smiling.

Cyrus Bascom glared at her, not letting go of the gun that remained fixed on Boyd.

Holly jabbed the broom handle in his back. "Give her the gun."

"Like hell I will," Bascom sneered. "Go ahead and shoot me. Go on. Shoot," he taunted. After a moment, he laughed. "You don't have the nerve."

As the sheriff started to turn, a voice came from behind.

"No, but I do." Nick Manelli stood in the kitchen doorway, his gun pointed at the sheriff. "Now, lower the gun and hand it to Kate."

The sheriff hesitated, then turned swiftly pointing his gun at Boyd. Holly screamed as a shot rang out. The sheriff fell to his knees and his gun dropped to the floor. Kate ran over and grabbed the gun, as the sheriff winced in pain using his left hand to cover the bullet hole Nick had put in his shooting hand.

“You all right?” he asked Holly, his gun still aimed at the sheriff.

Dropping the broom handle, she just nodded.

Kate walked over to where Boyd knelt by a canvas bag he’d been stuffing with plastic-wrapped white packets. He looked at her with a sheepish grin.

“This is one time I’m glad you’re a nosey neighbor, Kate.”

She smiled at him for a moment, then swiftly kicked him right between his legs causing him to howl as he fell on his back.

“That’s for Milly.” She stood over him, then delivered another kick to his ribs. “And that’s for Holly.”

Turning to face Holly and Nick, she grinned. “You saw him lunge at me, right?”

58 FORTY BUCKS

Holly yawned as she sat on a plastic chair in the corridor of State Police Headquarters in Liberty, NY. Feeling drained and sleepy, she wondered how much longer Kate's and Nick's interviews would take. Hers was pretty straightforward. She simply relayed what happened this morning. The trooper who interviewed her asked only a few questions and she was done.

She smiled remembering the scene in Milly Leggett's living room. Nick was right. She and Kate were crazy. But what else could they do? In spite of the fact that Boyd most probably was her kidnapper, she didn't think she'd ever get over it if he'd been murdered in cold blood as they sat cowering in the pantry cupboard.

At the sound of a door opening, Holly's eyes moved from the gleaming linoleum floor down the hallway. Kate headed towards her, an impish grin on her face.

"I actually enjoyed that," she said.

Holly gave her a weak smile, and Kate's expression grew serious.

“Hey, are you all right? You look awfully pale.”

“Just tired,” Holly replied.

Kate sank down beside her leaning her head against the wall. “Now that you mention it, I’m feeling a little fatigued myself. Must be post-adrenaline rush effects.” Sitting back up, she asked, “Where’s Nick?”

“He went in for his interview the same time as me and I haven’t seen him since.”

“They probably have a lot more questions for him than for us.” Kate leaned back again closing her eyes. “Was I ever glad to hear his voice back at Milly’s. He’s definitely my hero.”

“*My* hero, Kate,” Holly corrected.

Kate laughed. “What I don’t understand is how he always manages to show up just in the nick of time. How did he even know we were over at the Leggett’s?”

“I think his arriving at the Telicky house was pure luck. But I think Ivy was more responsible for his showing up today. I called her after my interview. She said that after they talked to Tommy, they were headed to Tommy’s friend’s house, but she got one of her ‘funny feelings’ and convinced Nick and Raquelle to stop at the house to check on us first.”

“Funny feeling?” Kate made quote marks in the air.

“Well, while I wouldn’t put us in the same psychic category as you and your grandmother, we do occasionally have these uncanny connections,” Holly explained. “I remember one time I was staying with a friend while my apartment was being painted. I had a nightmare that Ivy died in an accident. The next day I called her. She’d been trying to reach me for two days -- remember that was before cellphones and answering machines.”

"Ah, ancient America. Ouch," Kate said as Holly poked her in the ribs. "Still, how did Nick know we were next door?"

"Come on, Kate. He's a detective. Both our cars were in the driveway. When we weren't in the house or the yard, he knew where to look for us."

"Yeah, and then there was that police cruiser in the driveway."

"Yeah," Holly chuckled. "There was that."

After a moment, Kate said, "So you want to have your wedding in my backyard?"

"Whatever Nick wants," Holly replied.

"Listen to you!" Kate gave her a playful punch in the arm.

The two women just looked at one another and tears filled Holly's eyes. "We could have been killed, you know."

Kate put her arm around Holly's shoulder and squeezed. "But we weren't."

The friends sat in silence until a young trooper entered the corridor. As he approached them, he removed his hat revealing a marine-style haircut. His uniform looked crisp and unwrinkled, as if he'd just put it on.

"I'm Lieutenant Alex Cantrell, ladies. I'll be driving you back to Reddington Manor."

Holly stood up. "Where's Detective Manelli? Can't we see him before we leave?"

"If you'll follow me to the front desk, I'll check there Ma'am."

Holly and Kate followed the slim trooper down the hall. Stopping in the lobby, he said, "I'll be just a minute," as he walked over to the desk. The desk officer picked up a phone, then said something to the lieutenant.

"Ladies, you can have a seat. Detective Manelli will be out to talk to you shortly."

Holly sat down in a chair facing the front desk. "Thank heaven. I'd hate to leave here without seeing him."

Kate raised an eyebrow and smiled. Holly just rolled her eyes in reply.

When Nick appeared, Holly jumped up. She moved quickly across the lobby, put her head on his chest and began sobbing.

"Hey, what's wrong?" Nick put his muscular arms around her and looked over her head at Kate.

Kate shrugged. "Happy to see you, I guess."

Nick ran his hand along Holly's back and let her cry for a while. "It's okay," he soothed. "It's over."

Sniffling, Holly leaned back and looked up at him. "When we get home, I'm never leaving and I never want to see a dead body or a gun again as long as I live."

Nick gently brushed her tears away with his thumb. "No honeymoon?" he joked.

"Only if we go to a deserted island with no other possible murder victims."

Nick smiled at her. "You look exhausted. Go home and rest. I'll be there as soon as I'm finished here."

Holly frowned. "Why can't you come home with us now?"

"I want to be part of Boyd Leggett's interview."

Holly sighed as Nick turned to Lieutenant Cantrell. "Guard these ladies with your life,

Lieutenant. And no stops until you hand them over to her sister."

The trooper chuckled. "Yes, sir.

"I mean it," Nick said. "Do not stop with them for any reason. You have no idea what trouble they can get themselves into."

As Nick kissed Holly, Kate walked over to the trooper.

"Hey, Lieutenant. What does it take to get a marriage license in Sullivan County?" she asked

"All you need is $40 and proof of identification at the town clerk's office," he replied, holding open the door.

"You hear that, Nick?" Kate's devilish grin returned.

This time Holly rolled her whole head. Nick gave her a final squeeze, then looked at Kate. "I have to check, but I'm pretty sure I have my driver's license and 40 bucks on me."

59 INTERVIEW, PART ONE

In the hallway outside the interview room where Boyd Leggett waited, Major John Hodges stood facing Nick. The sixty-something officer had a crewcut Nick hadn't seen in years. His shirt collar screamed 'extra starch' and his shiny black boots looked as if they'd never been worn before today. In his hand, he held the folder on Boyd Leggett delivered from the Reddington Manor Police Department.

"Detective, I want you to know I still have misgivings about your participating in this interview."

Nick just nodded. He'd already done his best to show a totally dispassionate demeanor when he made the case for why he should be involved in questioning Boyd. He wasn't about to show any emotion now.

"Remember, if I determine that your personal involvement impairs your ability to question this suspect, I will stop the interview."

"Yes, sir," Nick replied. "I understand."

The major gave Nick one last assessing stare, then opened the door.

"Mr. Leggett, I'm Major Hodges and this is Detective Nick Manelli. I believe you met him earlier today."

Boyd's eyes darted from the major to Nick as they sat down across from him.

"Yeah," he replied, his apprehensive expression turning into a smile. "Yeah, you saved my life this morning." Boyd's half-hearted smile faded as he looked into Nick's impassive face.

Major Hodges opened the folder and began. "Mr. Leggett, you have quite a list of charges against you. Failure to report a death, government fraud, and kidnapping, and that doesn't even include today's charges of drug running and possibly bribery."

"Bribery? I never bribed anybody." Boyd appeared offended by the last charge.

"So, you're admitting you're guilty of all the other charges?" the major asked, glancing up from the papers on the table and focusing a penetrating stare at the hapless Boyd.

"No. Hell no," Boyd grasped the table. "I'm not guilty of any of that."

The major took a photo out of the folder and placed it directly in front of Boyd. "Mr. Leggett, this is a picture of you just a week ago at an ATM in Monticello making a withdrawal from your mother's checking account."

Boyd looked at the photo and fidgeted in his chair. "That ain't no crime. My mother gave me a bank card to her account. Said I could withdraw money if I needed it."

"The coroner determined that your mother was dead three months prior to that withdrawal."

"I -- uh -- I didn't know my mother had died."

Both the major and Nick just stared at Boyd.

"How was I supposed to know my mother was dead?"

"We have a neighbor who talked to you several times over the last three months who says you told her your mother was in rehab."

"Well, she's lying," Boyd said.

"We have two other witnesses who say they saw you at your mother's house on different occasions during the last three months."

"So? A son can't stop at his mother's house?"

The major leaned back in his chair and crossed his arms. "You stopped in your mother's house and when you didn't see her, you didn't wonder where she was? Didn't go upstairs to her bedroom to see if she was sick?"

"No, I figured she was out playing cards with her friends or at the supermarket." Boyd's eyes took on a reptilian appearance as he squirmed in his chair, causing it to squeak.

The major unfolded his arms and gave his head a slight shake as he turned over another sheet of paper in the file.

"We have another witness who saw you in your mother's house the night before she was kidnapped, held hostage for three days and found tied up in an abandoned house where she was left for dead."

"Maybe I was in the house, but you can't prove that I had anything to do with that kidnapping." It was Boyd's turn to sit back in his chair and fold his arms across his chest, a smug air about him.

"So you were upstairs in your mother's house and didn't notice her dead body?" the major asked without looking up.

Boyd's eyes widened. "I just said maybe I was in the house. But I wasn't, so nobody could've seen me."

"What do you think, Detective?" The major gave Nick a sideways glance.

Nick tilted his head in the major's direction, keeping his eyes on Boyd. Covering his mouth with his hand, he replied, "If I were the prosecutor, I think I'd load the jury with mothers."

"This ain't funny," Boyd sputtered as he grasped the table edges and leaned forward.

The major chuckled as he looked at his watch. "Time for a break, don't you think, Detective?"

The pair of lawmen stood up, looked at one another and burst out laughing as they left the room.

60 INTERVIEW, PART TWO

Back in his office, Major Hodges hung up the phone and looked at Nick. "That was Catskill Regional Medical Center. They said the bullet you put in the sheriff's hand has been removed, but he's being treated for shock and his doctor says he can't be questioned at least until tomorrow."

Nick shrugged and the major continued. "I suspect his lawyer had something to do with that course of treatment."

"I think you're right about that," Nick said. "I'm sure he and his lawyer are hard at work coming up with some alternative facts to explain what he was doing at the Leggett house this morning."

"Well, with your testimony, and the testimony of Ms. Donnelly and Ms. Farmer, I think even the wildest imagination is going to have trouble with that."

"Not to mention the testimony of our mother-loving, star witness, Boyd Leggett."

"Yep." The major stood up and headed to the door. "Any bets on how long it'll take for Boyd to turn state's evidence against the sheriff?"

Nick just smiled and followed the major back to the interview room. In the hallway, Hodges turned to him.

"Look, I had a hard time not reaching across the table and choking this guy before. Are you sure you can control yourself for the next part of this interview?"

"Absolutely," Nick said, opening the door for the trooper.

Inside the interview room, Nick grabbed a pen and legal pad from a shelf in the corner and sat down, burning Boyd with a focused stare. When Boyd started to squirm, he began.

"Tell us about what you were doing in your mother's house this morning, Mr. Leggett."

"Well, the sheriff called me and told me to meet him there. He told me he needed help with something."

"How did he get in touch with you?" Nick asked.

"He called me."

Nick jotted "APB" with a question mark on the legal pad and held it up for Major Hodges to see."

"Uh-huh," Hodges pursed his lips

"You have a cellphone?" Nick asked.

"Yeah -- no. I mean, it's my girlfriend's phone."

"That would be Roxy Barnett?"

"Yeah. How'd you know that?"

"Ms. Barnett contacted us at the recommendation of her lawyer," Nick lied. "Isn't that right, Major?"

The trooper crossed his arms and nodded.

“She’s on her way here now. We’ll be questioning her next,” Nick continued. “The kidnap victim says a young woman lured her to the back of the Main Street Deli the morning she was abducted. We’re going to see if she picks Ms. Barnett out of a line-up.”

Nick leaned back enjoying the moment. Boyd appeared stunned as the color drained from his face.

Nick turned to the trooper. “It’s okay if I share our next steps with Mr. Leggett, isn’t it Major?”

Hodges smiled and again nodded assent.

“After we interview Ms.Barnett, we’re going over to the hospital to interview Sheriff Bascom.” Nick leaned forward with a confidential air. “You know, Boyd -- it’s okay for me to call you Boyd? In the ambulance, the sheriff told State Troopers that he got a tip you were in the house and he went there to apprehend you.” Nick grimaced. “Now, I don’t know if we can believe him, but he said he thought you were going to pull a gun on us and that’s why he tried to shoot you.”

“Oh, hell no, he didn’t,” Boyd burst out. “Cyrus is nothing but a lying crook. He knew I didn’t have no gun.” He hit the table with clenched hands. “I’m not stupid. I know any crime carries a lot stiffer sentence if you carry a weapon. I told him from the start I wasn’t going to carry a gun, no matter what he had on me.”

Nick raised an eyebrow. “Are you saying the sheriff coerced you into committing a crime?”

Boyd paused, his mouth slowly forming a smile. “Yep. That’s exactly what I’m saying. I was coerced.” With a cocky toss of his head, he sat back in his chair.

"Okay, Boyd. We're going to need to know how Sheriff Bascom coerced you."

Jutting his chin out, Boyd looked from the major to Nick. "Look. I got a lot I can tell you about Cyrus Bascom, but I want something in return."

"Well, that's up to Major Hodges here," Nick said, deferring to the trooper at his side.

Hodges unfolded his arms and placed his palms on the table. "I assure you things will go better for you if we say you cooperated with us -- which up to now I can't say you have."

Boyd scratched his head, staring at the table. He appeared lost in thought. His two questioners made brief eye contact. Nick started to doodle on the legal pad as he waited for Boyd to arrive at the place he'd led him. Finally, Boyd looked up.

"Okay," he said. "I'll tell you everything."

61 HOMECOMING

Holly laughed watching Lucky, Amy and Winston tumble into one another as they chased the ball Benny threw to the back of Kate's yard. From her spot on the porch she could also see Razor as he spread the feed in the chicken coop. She recalled the day this unlikely twosome pulled into the driveway next door and felt a bit guilty about her initial assessment of them. Even though these guys didn't have conventional jobs, they put their lives on hold to help find her, then Boyd, even putting themselves in danger. How many people would do that she wondered.

"How you doing out there?" Ivy asked through the screen door.

"Never better," Holly replied. "How's it going *in there*?"

Ivy opened the door and stepped out onto the porch. "Everything's under control." She sank down onto the chair next to her sister. "I need a break."

"You know, after a little nap I'm really well enough to help." Holly turned towards Ivy.

"Not to worry. We're actually done. After you guys called from Liberty, Raquelle took me to the supermarket and the liquor store. She even helped me prepare the lasagna until she got the call to go downtown."

"God bless Nick's bail bondsman buddy," Holly smiled.

"Yeah, the lawyer he found managed to arrange for Tommy's release pretty quickly. He argued that there was no real evidence that Tommy committed the murder."

"I guess it didn't hurt that the arresting officer was now under arrest himself." Holly chuckled and looked out to the road. "I can't wait for everyone to get here."

"Me either," Kate said as she opened the door and joined the sisters on the porch. "All the finger foods and snacks are in serving bowls and all we have to do is put the lasagna in the oven as soon as Nick and Raquelle get back."

Holly looked at her watch. "He should be here soon."

"This was a great idea -- to have a wake for Milly and Chuck." Ivy looked at Kate.

"It was your sister's idea." Kate jutted her chin in Holly's direction.

"I should have known." Ivy grimaced. "She's big on wakes."

"Oh, come on," Holly said. "Besides, we also have cause to celebrate. Boyd and Bascom are in jail and Tommy's being released."

"Hear, Hear!" Kate said turning back to the door. "This calls for a toast. No reason we can't have a libation while we're waiting."

"That's right." Ivy jumped up and followed Kate into the kitchen.

Holly nestled into the chaise cushions with a contented sigh. Listening to the sounds of the glasses tinkling as Kate and Ivy got the drinks, she resumed watching Benny and the dogs play. Apparently he was as tireless as the three canines.

Holly sat up at the sound of a car engine in the distance. She looked to the road, hoping to see Nick's car. Instead the red Honda appeared. She got up and walked out to greet Raquelle and Tommy.

The sandy-haired boy gave Holly a huge grin as he got out of the car. The two embraced in a long hug.

"You saved my life," Holly said, her eyes glistening.

"No biggee," the boy replied as Benny, Razor and the canine trio arrived.

"Hey, man. Good to see you," Benny extended his hand to Tommy as the dogs rushed around in an animated frenzy of welcome.

"Good to be seen," Tommy replied shaking first Benny's hand, then Razor's. Next, he bent down and petted the dogs, letting Amy lick his face.

"Hey, you guys," Kate yelled from the porch. "Come on in and get something to eat and drink."

Raquelle put an arm around her son. "Hungry?"

"Are you kidding?" Tommy kissed her on the cheek and ran to the porch. "You got Twizzlers and Reese Cups for dessert?" he asked Kate as he gave her a hug.

"A whole bowlful," Kate replied returning the hug.

As the others reached the porch, Holly turned at the sound of another car coming up the road. "Oh, great," she said. "This must be Nick.

Everyone turned in time to see Flo's Kia pull into the driveway next door.

"Oh, Kate," Benny said sheepishly. "I forgot to tell you -- uh -- we ran into Flo downtown on our way back this afternoon."

62 THE WAKE

"Why don't you all go inside?" Kate held the door open as the group filed in. Holly remained standing by her.

"Hi, Flo," she greeted as the big woman lumbered over carrying a canvas shopping tote. "Glad you could make it."

"Oh, sure," Flo used the banister to pull herself up the steps. "I wouldn't want to miss this." Handing the tote bag to Kate, she chortled. "Here. Thought you'd want these. Picked them up today just for the occasion. You can keep them."

Flo waddled through the door as Holly and Kate peered inside the bag and saw a black ceramic urn.

"Chuck is definitely in a better place," Kate whispered.

Holly gave a weary nod and the pair followed the others inside. Ivy had already guided the guests into the dining room and was placing the lasagna in the oven.

"What's that?" she asked.

"Chuck's ashes," Holly whispered in her ear.

Ivy smiled grimly. "Well, then, let's go join the guests."

In the dining room, Flo loaded her plate. "Nice spread you got here, Kate. But don't tell me you don't have anything stronger to drink than wine and beer. I know you always kept a bottle of Jack Daniels for when Chuck came over. Where is it?"

"Aunt Flo!" Benny looked shocked. "You could be a little more gratuitous to our hostess."

"Gracious," Razor said.

"I swear, you sound just like your Uncle Chuck, boy." Flo glared at Benny. "And he's just your uncle by marriage. I'm your blood relative."

"I'll get the Jack Daniels." Kate quickly moved between Benny and Flo. "You want ice with that, Flo?"

Flo's expression softened just a bit. "Yeah, that'd be nice," she said, walking through the archway into the living room, dropping onto the couch. Benny followed Kate into the kitchen.

"Sorry, Kate," he said. "This is my fault. Razor always tells me 'loose lips sink ships'. Wish I was more like him."

Kate smiled as she reached in the cupboard for the bottle of Jack Daniels. "Then you wouldn't be you and I'd be sorry." Grabbing a glass, she filled it with ice and said, "Don't worry about it. C'mon."

Benny frowned as he trailed behind her back into the dining room where he stood as far away from Flo as possible.

"I hear Cyrus is in the hoosegow," Flo said as Kate handed her the ice filled glass. "That's what he gets for trusting a bum like Boyd Leggett." Before Kate could unscrew the top of the liquor bottle, Flo grabbed it from her hand. "Here, I'll take care of that."

Kate turned and quickly retrieved her wine glass from where she'd left it on the dining room table. Lifting the glass, she took a long draught. After a moment, she turned to face the group. "I'd like to say a few words." Ignoring Flo's grunt, she looked around the room.

"Thank you all for coming. I just wanted to do something to honor the memory of our friends who are no longer with us. Milly Leggett was a good neighbor to me. She taught me a lot about gardening in the Catskills when I first moved here. I will always remember her sweet, smiling face." Raising her glass, she said, "To Milly".

Everybody raised their glasses, echoing her words. After everyone took a drink, Kate continued.

"Next, I will miss my other good neighbor, Chuck Dwyer. Chuck was always there to lend a helping hand, like when my water heater exploded, and when I couldn't get the car out of the garage, and…"

"Where's the urn?" Flo cut in as she poured herself another glass of Jack.

"Oh," Kate paused, looking uncertain.

"I'll get it." Holly disappeared into the kitchen returning with the tote bag. She held it open and Ivy pulled the urn out, placing it on the side table next to the vase of gladiolas.

"Thank you," Kate said, staring at the urn. After a moment, she looked back up. "As I was saying, Chuck was a good neighbor and a friend indeed. To Chuck."

"To Chuck," the group said in unison. Everyone remained silent for a bit, the party atmosphere abated, when Flo suddenly got up from the couch.

"My turn," she said. "I can't say I'll miss Chuck, and I can't wait until I forget the way he looked in that blood-soaked red, flannel shirt I always hated. He wasn't the best husband in the world, but I guess he wasn't the worst either. To Chuck." Raising her glass to her mouth, she emptied it, and banged the glass down on the coffee table. "Okay, I had enough of this pity party."

Abruptly the big woman turned and headed to the kitchen. A wide-eyed Kate ran after her.

"Thanks for coming, Flo."

"Yeah, yeah," Flo said as she walked out the door into the night air.

Before she got in the Kia, Nick's car pulled in. Kate watched through the screen door as he got out of the car, surprised to see someone getting out of the passenger side as well.

"Hope you don't mind, Kate. I invited Jason."

"No, of course not. I'm glad you could join us Jason," she said opening the door. In the kitchen, the stove timer started beeping. "Perfect timing, you guys. The lasagna is ready." She turned off the oven and grabbed the hot pads.

"Smells like heaven in here," Nick said.

"Italian heaven anyway." Kate laughed pointing to the dining room. "Beer and wine is through that doorway," she said.

Holly smiled when she spotted Nick. Setting her drink down on the table, she put her arms around his waist and hugged him. "I'm so glad you're here. I was beginning to worry."

"I told you, you never have to worry about me." He gave her a kiss and reached for the beer Razor handed him.

"What the hell are you doing here?"

A hush fell over the room as Jason appeared to whither under Raquelle's glare.

63 DISSEMBLE

"Mom!" Tommy put his plate on the coffee table and stood beside his mother. "Come sit back down," he said, gently tugging on her arm.

Raquelle's glare disappeared as she looked at her son. Nodding, she walked over to the couch and sat down in the spot Flo had vacated.

"Jason, you want a beer?" Benny asked, holding up a Michelob Ultra can.

Jason looked at Benny, appearing uncertain. "No, thanks. I think I better go."

Nick looked at Holly. She recognized the silent plea for help. Detaching herself from him, she walked over and laced her arm through Jason's. As she led him to the table, she said softly, "Please stay. At least have a beer and something to eat before you go."

Jason appeared reluctant. After a glance at Nick, he finally nodded. Benny pulled the top off the beer can and handed it to him.

"You know my friend, Razor?" Benny asked as he clinked his beer can against Jason's.

"Okay, everybody," Kate said as she entered the dining room carrying the baking dish of steaming lasagna. "As Lidia says '*Tutti a tavola a mangiare*!'

"I sure hope that means 'come and get it'," Benny said, picking up a plate.

"Actually, that's a pretty good translation," Kate laughed.

Ooohs, aahhs and laughter followed as she placed the dish in the middle of the table and everyone grabbed a plate and got in line behind Benny.

****

Nick returned with his third helping and sat down in a folding chair beside Holly's. "What are you smiling about?" he asked as he lifted another forkful of lasagna to his mouth.

"This is just so wonderful, isn't it? I mean, just a few days ago, I..." She choked up, unable to finish the sentence.

Nick leaned over and kissed her. "Here. Have some more lasagna, he said, offering her his fork. "It's almost as good as yours."

"You always know the right thing to say." Holly laughed as she took a bite.

Suddenly, Benny's voice grew louder. "Hey, tell me I'm wrong. Look at these two guys." Benny was pointing at Jason and Tommy who were standing side by side at the table. "Don't they dissemble one another?"

"Benny," Razor shook his head as he stared at his friend, this time not correcting his error.

Benny said, "What? Really they look enough alike to be father and..." Benny hesitated and looked around the room, stopping when his eyes reached

Raquelle. "Oops," he said, picking up his beer and heading to the kitchen.

All conversation ceased as Jason and Tommy stood staring at one another. Raquelle got up from the couch. "Tommy, let's go," she said.

The boy turned to his mother. "Is he my father?"

"Let's go," she snapped and stormed past everyone into the kitchen and out the back door.

Tommy turned to Jason. "Are you my father?"

Jason look stunned. "I don't know."

"*Could* you be my father?" the boy asked.

Jason stared at Tommy. After a moment, his expression turned to one of resolve. "Yeah. Yeah, I could be. Let's go talk to your mother."

As the two men left the room, Razor sighed loudly as he shook his head. "Benny."

Kate patted Razor on his bulging forearm. "This could be a good thing." She walked over to the table, picked up the empty lasagna dish and handed it to him. She grabbed the salad bowl.

"Yeah," Ivy said, picking up some empty dishes, "especially if he is Tommy's father. I'm surprised no one else ever noticed the resemblance."

Kate, Razor and Ivy carried the dishes into the kitchen leaving Holly and Nick alone.

"You knew, didn't you?" Holly asked.

"Naw," Nick took another swig of beer. "What?" he asked as Holly continued to stare at him. "Okay. I didn't realize Tommy might be his son, but the two times I saw Raquelle and Jason interact, I knew there was history between them."

Holly giggled. "So now you're a matchmaker."

“No, no,” Nick shook his head. “There’s only one match I’m interested in making. What do you say we go upstairs and work on that?”

As they stood up, Ivy returned to the dining room. “Hey, you two, come on outside. We’re having a nightcap on the porch. It’s beautiful out.”

Kate stuck her head in the door. “Yeah, we’ve got some questions for you, Detective.”

“We’ll be right out,” Holly said. An apologetic look on her face, she put her arms around his waist. “We’ve got all night.”

“All night. Sounds good to me,” Nick said as they headed to the back door.

64 POST-MORTEM

Outside Razor sat on the steps. Winston lay beside him with his head resting on the big man's thigh. Benny perched on the banister and Kate and Ivy sat on the wicker chairs waiting for Nick and Holly.

"Here," Ivy patted the cushions. "We saved the love seat for you two." She grinned as she pronounced the word 'love' in two syllables.

Holly reduced her eyes to slits looking down at her sister. "Really, Ivy?" she said as she lowered herself onto the cushions.

"What happened to Jason?" Nick asked as he dropped down beside her.

"Last I saw, him and Tommy were walking up the road," Benny replied.

"What about Raquelle? Holly asked.

"Well, she got in her car, and told Tommy to get in. I couldn't hear what he said to her, but she looked real mad. She burnt rubber pulling out of the driveway and drove up to her house." Benny frowned. "Geez, I didn't realize what I was saying until it was too late."

"Big surprise." Razor patted Winston's head.

"Oh, c'mon," Benny protested. "Maybe I did a good thing this time. You guys think they'll get together?"

"I don't hear any shouting." Kate looked up the road towards Raquelle's house. "That's a good sign. That means they're talking."

Ivy suddenly turned to Nick. "Wait a minute. Did you invite Jason tonight because you suspected Tommy was his son?"

"No. I invited him because I stopped at the police station on my way back from Liberty. He was packing up some stuff. Until the State Troopers complete the investigation and clear him of any connection to his uncle's wrongdoings, he's on an administrative suspension. I felt sorry for him."

Holly poked Nick in the ribs. "Admit it. You suspected they had some kind of a relationship."

"Well, yeah," Nick said putting his arm around Holly. "A woman doesn't talk tough to a man the way Raquelle did to Jason unless she loves him." With his free arm, Nick prevented Holly from swatting him.

"Amen," Razor said softly.

"Whoa ho!" Benny guffawed. "You got that right, Nick."

"I don't believe you guys!" Holly struggled to get loose from Nick's grip, but finally just relaxed into it.

When Ivy stopped giggling she asked, "So, Nick, you don't think Jason was involved in his uncle's crimes, do you?"

"I can't be sure," Nick answered. "He might have suspected the sheriff of shady dealings and just looked the other way. After all Bascom was not just his boss, he was family. Still, I don't think Jason's a dirty cop."

"Okay," Kate said. "Enough about them. Here's what I want to know. Did Boyd confess?"

"Yes and no," Nick replied. "The sheriff caught him stealing from the liquor store one night and used that as leverage to get Boyd to transport drugs around the county."

"No way!" Benny exclaimed. "And he's our sheriff?"

"Yep. Boyd also confessed to the kidnapping when I said his girlfriend was coming in and Holly would be able to pick her out of a line up as the woman who lured her into the alley behind the deli."

"Do I have to do that?" Holly asked, moving to the edge of her seat.

"Probably, but relax." Nick circled the back of her neck with his hand. "It's not a big deal, and I'll be with you."

Holly frowned as she nestled back into his embrace.

"But why did he take Holly in the first place?" Ivy asked.

"He said when she spotted him in the house that night, he got worried. The room he was in was his mother's, so there was no way he could deny knowing she was dead and that he would be charged with bank fraud. He also said he was supposed to get enough money from this last haul of cocaine for him and Roxy to leave town."

"So he just needed her out of the way until he could transport the drugs and get his money," Kate summarized.

"How did he defend leaving her tied up in an abandoned house?" Ivy asked.

"He claimed he was going to have Roxy call Kate and tell her where Holly was, but that got delayed. Cyrus wasn't going to give him his money until he made the delivery. Even with the sheriff running interference for him, he was afraid of being spotted by someone else if he returned to the house."

"So if they hadn't kidnapped me, and we left with Kate for New Jersey, they would have been able to get in the house and would have gotten away with it."

"Probably." Nick nodded.

"But here's what I really want to know." Kate said. "Did he confess to killing Chuck?"

"No, and I honestly don't think he did it," Nick answered.

"Really?" Kate tilted her head. "I was sure it had to be him."

"He opened up about everything, when he realized what we had on him, but he was adamant about not killing Chuck. He also said he never carried a weapon because he knew committing a crime with one resulted in a much longer jail sentence."

"Do you think Bascom killed Chuck?" Kate asked.

"Don't know. Maybe. " Nick shrugged.

The porch grew quiet as everybody seemed to get lost in their own thoughts. Finally, Razor stood up.

"Thanks for the great food and drink, Kate," he said.

Benny slid off the banister. "Yeah. Everything was terrific. I'm really sorry about inviting Aunt Flo."

Kate laughed. "Yeah, we probably could have done without that toast of hers."

"Hmpf." Benny put his hands on his hips. "You know, something's been bothering me about that." He looked out into the night sky. Snapping his fingers, he looked back at Kate. "I know. The day after Uncle Chuck was murdered, I remember telling Aunt Flo how sorry I was. I said it must have been hard for her to identify Uncle Chuck's body down at the morgue. She laughed at me and said she didn't have to. That *you* did that, Kate."

"That's right," Kate said.

"Then how come tonight she said she couldn't wait to forget seeing him in his bloody, red flannel shirt?"

"Oh, my God!" Kate gasped.

Nick stood up and pulled out his cellphone. "Major Hodges, please."

65 LINE-UP

Monday morning Nick held Holly's hand as she viewed a line-up of women through the two-way mirror at State Trooper Headquarters in Liberty.

"Number 3," she said. "That's definitely the girl who told me to go to the back of the deli."

Lieutenant Cantrell spoke into the microphone. "Number three, step forward."

The woman wearing the number three on her chest frowned, put her head down and took a step forward. A trooper walked over and handed her a card.

Almost inaudibly, the young woman read the text.

"Louder," Cantrell barked.

"Get up. I'm taking you to the bathroom," the woman read.

"Oh yeah," Holly said. "That was the woman in the witch's mask."

"Okay," Cantrell said into the microphone, clicking the sound system off. " You did great, Ms. Donnelly."

"What's going to happen to her?" Holly asked.

"She'll be arrested and charged as an accessory to kidnapping. She doesn't have a record. If she can provide any testimony that will help us convict Sheriff Bascom, she may get off with a light sentence." The lieutenant held the door open for them. "You know your way out, right?"

Nick nodded. After shaking hands, Cantrell turned and headed in the opposite direction. As they walked to the lobby, Nick asked, "You don't feel sorry for her, do you?"

Holly laughed. "What, are you worried I'm re-opening the Holly Donnelly Home for Wayward Girls?"

"That wouldn't totally surprise me," he said squeezing her hand.

"You can stop worrying. That young woman needs a good time out to think about what she's done."

A voice called from down the hall. "Detective Manelli."

Nick and Holly turned to see Major Hodges approaching.

"How'd it go?" he asked.

"Not bad," Holly replied. "The woman I saw at the deli was in the line-up and when she spoke I recognized her voice. She definitely was the woman who held me hostage."

"Good," Hodges nodded.

"How'd the interview with Bascom go?" Nick asked.

The major chuckled, "Not as well as he hoped. You'll be interested to know he said exactly what you told Boyd he would -- that he got an anonymous tip that Boyd was at the house and he only tried to shoot him because he thought he was about to shoot you all. You could have been a great defense attorney, Detective."

"No thanks," Nick laughed. "As a matter of fact, I'm considering settling down to a peaceful life of retirement."

Holly's eyes widened, but she said nothing.

"What about the Dwyer woman?" Nick asked.

"Oh," Hodges shook his head. "What a piece of work that one is. First, she tried to say she must have dreamt about the red flannel shirt. Then she said Ms. Farmer must have told her about it. Doesn't matter what she says. Our search of her sister's place found a bloody shirt and pair of pants in the garbage. I just got the call confirming it was Mr. Dwyer's blood."

"Wow, I didn't much like her, but I can't believe she killed her husband with his own meat cleaver." Holly shivered.

"Actually that's probably the only thing she's got going for her," Nick said. "If she didn't bring the meat cleaver with her, her lawyer will argue it was a crime of passion and not premeditated."

"But she knocked him out first," Holly argued.

Nick shook his head. "They'll argue that in a fit of passion, she grabbed the cleaver and just swung wildly. She'll say she didn't realize what she'd done until the cleaver got stuck in Chuck's chest."

"Ew!" Holly shivered again.

The major chuckled. "Like I said, you would have made a great defense attorney, Detective. Glad you're on our side." Looking from Nick to Holly, he said, "Seriously, I want to thank you both for all you did here. You helped us solve a murder and prevent a shipment of cocaine from hitting the streets. We've suspected for some time that someone in law enforcement was aiding the Monticello drug dealers, but we had no idea who it was. I'm sorry for all you've been through, Ms. Donnelly, but I'm certainly glad of the outcome."

"Me too," Holly said.

"Major," the receptionist called out. "Judge Malcom on the phone for you."

"Duty calls," Hodges said. "Get home safe now."

Outside, Holly asked, "Were you serious about retirement?"

"Thinking about it," Nick said as he opened the car door for her.

Instead of getting in, she stood looking up at him.

"What?" he smiled. "Taking care of you is a full time job, you know."

"Very funny," she said.

"Get in." Nick looked at his watch. "We have just enough time."

"Just enough time for what?" she asked as he guided her into the seat and closed the door.

When Nick got in the driver side, she asked again, "Just enough time for what?

"To get to the county clerk's office before they go to lunch."

"Why are we going to the…" Holly stopped and swallowed hard.

Nick grinned as he turned the key in the ignition. "You told me to name the date. Today's the day."

66 TWENTY-FOUR HOURS

Lucky, Amy and Winston ran to the driveway as Holly and Nick pulled up. They repeated their customary frenetic welcome, but Lucky seemed especially happy to see the pair. Nick bent down and rubbed her ears.

"Good girl!" he said. "When we get home, I'm going to fix this dog a steak dinner. With all that's been going on, I don't think she's gotten the hero treatment she deserves."

"I'm all for that." Holly knelt down beside the dog and hugged her neck. Standing back up, she smiled. "Home. That sounds so good. It was great having the weekend to just laze around and catch up, but I am ready to go home."

"Yeah, I've had enough of the country life myself." Nick pulled her close. "But let's get one thing straight. We still have a lot of catching up to do."

Holly smiled. "Save something for the honeymoon."

Giving him a quick kiss, she took Nick's hand and pulled him towards the house. As they neared the porch, they heard laughter inside. At the sound of the door, Kate, Ivy, Benny and Tommy turned in unison.

"Oh, you're just in time," Ivy chuckled. "Benny's been telling us about his family's reaction to Flo's arrest."

"Yeah," Benny's grin evaporated. "But listen, before I say anything, I need you to swear you will never tell a soul that I'm the one that caught Aunt Flo's lie or anything else I'm about to tell you."

Holly and Nick both raised their right hands and simultaneously said, "I swear."

"Okay." Benny crouched in a conspiratorial posture. "The only reason they found Aunt Flo's bloody shirt was because nobody in the darn house took the garbage out. I usually stop by once a week to do that for my mother, but with everything that's been going on, I didn't get there this week."

"So you're single-handedly responsible for solving your Uncle Chuck's murder and getting me completely off the hook," Tommy said.

"That must make you feel good." Holly patted Benny on the shoulder.

"Honestly, I have what you call mixed demotions." Benny's expression turned glum. "I'm glad we know who did it and we don't have to worry there's some crazed killer out there. But I do feel a little bad about Aunt Flo. Maybe if things had worked out for her and Bascom, she'd have had a better life."

"What!" Kate exclaimed. "She and the sheriff had a thing?"

"Oh, boy," Benny muttered. "There I go again. Telling secrets."

"I knew there had to be a connection between those two." Kate lightly pounded the table with her fist. "Dish, Benny!"

Benny grimaced. "I thought everyone knew. They were king and queen of the prom in high school."

"Wow," Ivy gasped. "I can't picture Flo as prom queen."

"Oh, yeah," Benny said. "She was a real looker. My mom has pictures."

"What happened between them?" Tommy asked.

"From what my mother says, Aunt Flo had a temper even back then. One night she and Bascom had a big fight out in the parking lot at a bar. He slapped her around, and Uncle Chuck stopped him. The rest is history."

"You're kidding?" Kate said.

Benny shook his head. "Nope. And I always felt like Bascom still had a thing for Aunt Flo. It's really kind of sad. And now she's going to jail and it's all my fault."

Nick put his hand on Benny's shoulder. "No, it's not your fault. She murdered her husband. You're not responsible. Besides, you should be looking on the bright side. After everything that's happened, you could have a future in law enforcement."

"Aw, go on." Benny blushed.

"Yeah," Kate said. "We are going to need a new sheriff now that Bascom's in jail."

"No, no." Benny shook his whole body. "That ain't the life for me."

"Seriously. What about private detective work?" Ivy asked.

The kitchen door opened again and Razor walked in. "I heard what you said, little sister. Mr. Loose Lips here could never be a private eye."

"Razor's right." Benny nodded in agreement. "We got our own odd job business and that's good enough for me."

Kate turned to Nick and Holly. "So how'd it go in Liberty?"

"I picked Roxy Barnett out of the line-up and as soon as she read a sentence, I knew she was the woman in the witch's mask."

"Aren't you going to tell them?" Nick looked at Holly.

"I'll let you tell them," Holly replied smiling.

"Well, tell us already," Kate said waving her hands impatiently.

"We stopped at the county clerk's office and got a marriage license."

"Oh, how wonderful!" Ivy jumped out of her chair and ran over to hug Holly.

"About time," Kate said, walking over to the refrigerator. Pulling out a bottle of Perrier-Jouet, she said, "Tommy, could you get the champagne flutes out of the cabinet in the dining room." She handed the bottle to Nick. "You know how long I've been waiting for this?"

"Not as long as me," he laughed, pulling the paper off the bottle top and popping the cork.

Tommy placed the glasses on the counter as Kate poured. When everyone had a glass in hand, Kate raised hers. "To Holly and Nick. May you live happily ever after."

"To Holly and Nick," everyone repeated.

"Oh, this is going to be great," Ivy gushed. "Maybe I can stay a few more days when we get back to New Jersey and help you start planning the wedding."

Holly grimaced. “Well, we don’t really want a wedding.”

“Yeah,” Nick said. “If the Justice of the Peace weren’t in Binghamton today, we’d already be married.”

“What!” Ivy put her glass down. “No, no! You have to have a wedding.”

“Oh, yeah,” Kate said. “You’re not depriving me of this.”

“Well, if you want a wedding, you’re going to have to plan it in the next twenty-four hours,” Nick said. “I left my number for the Justice of the Peace and told him to call me about marrying us tomorrow.”

Kate and Ivy made eye contact. “We can do that.”

67 BACK STORY

On the porch, Holly, Ivy and Kate all stopped and stared at one another as the theme song from Rocky poured out of Holly's cellphone. Ivy held up crossed fingers on both hands as Holly answered.

"Yeah. Uh-huh. Okay. I love you." She broke into a smile as she looked at her sister and her friend. "Looks like it's a go. Nick says the Justice of the Peace can make it here tomorrow at two o'clock."

Kate and Ivy squealed as they gave each other high fives.

"Okay, we can cross that off the list." Kate picked up her pen and made a mark on her legal pad as the red Honda pulled into the driveway.

They heard the sound of the trunk pop before Raquelle opened her door.

"Oh, let's see what she's got." Ivy rushed down the steps and across the yard.

By the time Holly and Ivy got to the car, Raquelle was handing bags to Ivy.

"I got dinner rolls, plastic plates, silverware, cups and napkins. The restaurant said they can have the food and cake delivered by one-thirty tomorrow. If that's good, I'll call and confirm the order right now."

"Make the call," Kate said. "We just got word that the Justice of the Peace will be here at two."

"This is so exciting," Ivy said as they carried the bags inside. "Everything is just coming together perfectly."

After Raquelle completed the call, she said, "Okay. Anything else you want me to do?"

Kate looked down at her legal pad, and then back up grinning. "I think you can relax, now. You've helped whittle our to-do list down considerably."

"We can't thank you enough," Ivy said.

"Okay, then." Raquelle smiled. "I'm going home."

She headed out the door and Kate quickly followed.

"Wait, Raquelle. Why don't you sit down. I'll get you some iced tea. Are you hungry?"

As Holly and Ivy stepped out on the porch, Raquelle gave Kate a wary look. "You just want to know what happened with me and Jason last night."

Kate filled her cheeks with air, then exhaled loudly. "Guilty as charged."

"Not just Kate," Ivy added. "I'm curious, too."

"You might as well sit down and tell us," Holly said as she sat down on the chaise. "They won't stop hounding you until you do. Believe me, I know what I'm talking about. And you don't want to have this conversation tomorrow during the wedding reception."

Raquelle dropped into a chair. "Okay, here's the back story. Jason and I had a brief fling the summer after graduation. Then, one day, I find out he's left for Europe without even saying good-bye. After that he went off to college without ever coming home." She looked out across the yard. "He broke my heart."

Ivy sat in the chair next to Raquelle and patted her forearm. "And Tommy?"

Raquelle lowered her eyes to the floor. After a moment, she looked up. "Oh, what the hell! After last night it doesn't matter anymore. Damn Benny! Yes, Jason is Tommy's father."

"He never knew?" Holly asked.

"No."

"And you never tried to contact him?" Kate said.

"Oh, I went by his house once that summer. His mother called me a tramp and said I had a lot of nerve coming to her front door -- that Jason was out of my league and if I knew what was good for me, I'd never come around again."

"The whole Bascom family sounds just darling," Holly scoffed.

"What did Jason have to say for himself?" Ivy asked.

"He said one morning he woke up, his bags were packed and his Uncle Cyrus said the trip to Europe was his surprise graduation present. When he flew back, Cyrus picked him up at the airport and drove him straight to his college dorm at the University of South Carolina. He claims he looked for me when he came home at Christmas, but by then I was gone."

"Where'd you go?" Kate asked.

"When I told my mother I was pregnant, she threw me out. I went and stayed with my aunt in Binghamton until Tommy was born. I was going to stay there, but then my mother died and I inherited the house, so I came back here. I should have sold the damn place and stayed with my aunt, but no. Not me. I had to prove something." Raquelle lowered her head.

"I get that," Holly sat forward in her chair. "Don't beat yourself up."

"Did you hope Jason would maybe come around?" Ivy asked.

"At first." Raquelle's expression hardened. "But that got old fast. I had a son to take care of. I'm not proud of everything I did back then, but I made sure Tommy was fed and healthy. I slept with anyone who could help me keep the roof over our heads. That's when Cyrus came sniffing around."

"Oh, gosh." Kate's eyes widened. "I forgot you told us Cyrus Bascom pressured you to have sex with him."

"I think he suspected Tommy was Jason's. I guess he just wanted to drive me out of town. When I turned him down, he started to harass the men I was involved with -- threatening to arrest them on some trumped up charge." Raquelle's angry face transformed into a wicked smile. "That's when I finally smartened up."

"What did you do?" Ivy asked.

"I had an affair with then Mayor Bobby Crenshaw."

"You didn't!" Kate giggled.

"I told you I'm not proud of everything I did back then, but Crenshaw got me the job with the parks commission and got Cyrus Bascom off my back. Life was real good until Bobby died two years ago." The clouds returned to Raquelle's brow. "That's when Cyrus started harassing Tommy."

"Well, you don't have to worry about that anymore," Holly said. "From what Nick told me, they've got him on everything from drug-running to coercion and evidence tampering."

Ivy looked wistful. "What's Jason's side of this? He never suspected Tommy was his son?"

Raquelle sighed. "After college he got married to Ashley Brenner -- the Brenners own half of Reddington Manor. She was his mother's dream choice for her son." Raquelle rolled her eyes. "By then, my reputation was pretty well shot. He said he heard I'd sleep with anybody who'd pay the electric bill, so he never thought Tommy was his son. He said whenever he tried to approach me, I treated him like dirt. That part is true."

Kate's brow creased. "Didn't I hear he got divorced?"

Raquelle just nodded.

"Any chance you two might have a future together?" Ivy asked.

"Stop." Holly snapped, turning to Raquelle. "Don't let them make you crazy."

"Ignore her." Kate gave Holly a dismissive wave. "How's Tommy dealing with all this?"

Raquelle shook her head, a half-frown, half-smile on her face. "Well, that's just it. He and Jason seem to have bonded instantly. Tonight, they're meeting for pizza downtown and they're planning a fishing trip next weekend. Jason has two daughters, so he seems just thrilled to have a son to do guy things with."

"Aw, that's great." Ivy smiled.

Holly's left eyebrow popped upward. "Looks like you're going to have some kind of relationship with Jason, like it or not."

"Looks like," Raquelle nodded.

"Well, if you need help planning a wedding…"

68 AT LAST

"You look beautiful." Ivy beamed at Holly.

Holly looked in the mirror. "Not bad. Can you believe Kate actually bought this dress for herself? I'm two sizes bigger than her and it fits me perfectly."

Over Holly's shoulder, Ivy admired her sister's reflection in the mirror. The champagne pink dress flattered Holly's curves.

"It's not really her style either."

"Okay," Kate rushed into the room carrying a bouquet of flowers. Stopping as Holly turned to face her, she said, "Oh, the dress is perfect. It fits as if it was made for you."

"Yes," Ivy said. "We were wondering whatever possessed you to buy this dress. It's not your size or your style."

Kate tilted her head, a Mona Lisa smile on her face. "You know, I'm not sure. I didn't even try it on. I just remember feeling that I had to buy it."

"Do you think your grandmother had something to do with that?" Holly asked.

Kate laughed. "Possibly, but you know this wouldn't be the first time I bought something not knowing why and then months later found a use for it."

"You're a little scary." Ivy walked over and hugged Kate. "But I've grown to love you as much as Holly does."

"Stop," Holly said, "before I get misty-eyed and ruin my make-up. Let me see that bouquet."

"You like?" Kate held the bouquet out for the sisters to examine.

"Magnificent!" Holly said. "Now I know, everything in this bouquet has to have a meaning. Of course, I know the red roses symbolize love."

"The arbor is so loaded with roses, you can't even notice I removed these. The best part is they're in full bloom today."

"That's a good omen," Ivy nodded.

"Oh, look, Ivy!" Holly exclaimed. "She put in some holly branches and ivy vines."

"But, of course," Kate grinned. "Holly is for domestic happiness and ivy is for wedded love and fidelity. I also threw in some lavender for devotion, parsley for festivity and I couldn't leave out baby's breath."

"I know that one," Ivy said. "That's for everlasting love."

"Thank you, Kate." Holly took the bouquet in her arms. "You, too, Ivy. I didn't want a wedding, but what you've managed to accomplish in twenty-four hours is just amazing. And I love everything you've done."

"Yes, I'm pretty proud of us." Kate nodded.

A car horn caused Kate to go to the window. “The food is here. I better go downstairs.”

“I’ll go,” Ivy volunteered. “Don’t you think you should get dressed?”

Kate looked down at her grass-stained jeans. “Oh, yeah.”

****

Centered under the arbor, the Justice of the Peace closed his book and smiled. “I pronounce you husband and wife. You may now kiss the bride.”

Nick met no resistance as he pulled Holly close and kissed her. As everyone applauded, he whispered in her ear. “I love you.”

“I love you more,” she whispered back.

The newlyweds turned to the group patiently waiting to congratulate them.

Kate hugged Holly. “Now, don’t screw this up.”

Holly looked at her friend with a droll smile. “You couldn’t just say congratulations?”

“Aw, you don’t want me to get sappy, do you?” Kate squeezed Holly’s arms and released her. “I’ve got to go help Raquelle and Tommy pour the champagne,” she said as she scurried off in the direction of the porch.

As Ivy hugged Holly, Benny shook Nick’s hand. “Way to go, Nick.”

“Good luck, man,” Razor smiled as he congratulated the groom. “You got your hands full now.”

“Champagne is now being served,” Kate called from the porch.

Razor and Benny immediately headed in that direction.

Jason shook Nick's hand last.

"Congratulations."

"You next?" Nick grinned.

Jason smiled and shrugged. "I don't know. Maybe." As the two men turned and started slowly towards the house, he added. "I want to thank you."

"For what?" Nick asked

"For everything. I've been reinstated. Major Hodges told me your endorsement was a big part of their decision to repeal my suspension."

"You did your best to help me." Nick frowned. "I am sorry about your uncle."

"Yeah. Me too. In spite of all he's done, he did keep me out of it. But he's also the one who gave me the surprise trip to Europe the summer before I left for college. I realize now he did it to break me and Raquelle up. My mother didn't approve of her. I never got to say good-bye. I didn't know she was pregnant or…" Jason paused.

"Things are good with you two now?" Nick asked.

"Yeah," Jason nodded. "I think so."

"Nick, we're waiting for you," Kate shouted.

The men picked up their pace and Nick mounted the steps two at a time. Tommy handed each a champagne flute and Kate tapped her glass with a spoon.

"Okay, everyone. Ivy is going to make the toast."

Ivy raised her glass. "To my sister and my new brother. I can't think of any better words to say than the ones Kate said yesterday. May you both live happily ever after. To Holly and Nick."

The group echoed the toast and everyone took a drink.

Ivy and Kate walked over to Holly and all three clinked glasses and held them high.

"Oh my goodness!" Ivy stopped, a look of wonderment on her face.

"What is it?" Holly asked.

"Do you remember the tarot reading Kate did? Remember the four cards underneath?"

"I do," Kate nodded grinning. "Today for sure we are the three woman rejoicing on that Three of Cups card."

"And wasn't there a wedding card?" Ivy asked.

Again, Kate nodded. "Oh, yeah. The Ten of Cups." She turned to face the group and said, "I have another toast to make. This is to the Empress and her King of Wands -- to Holly and Nick."

After everyone took another sip of champagne, Kate continued. "Even though this is not the most traditional wedding, Ivy and I decided you two should have a first dance and we picked the song that we think is just right for you."

She tapped the IPOD and the initial strains of "At Last" poured out of the speaker. As the instantly recognizable voice of Etta James began to croon, Nick took Holly in his arms and they began to sway to the music.

"You hear that? Nick whispered as the final words 'you're mine at last' ended the song. "How's it feel?"

"Like my lonely days are over." Holly smiled. "At last."

If you liked this book, please write a review on Amazon.com.

ABOUT THE AUTHOR

President of the Upstate South Carolina Chapter of Sisters in Crime (SinC), Sally Handley debuted her Holly and Ivy cozy mystery series with her first book, *Second Bloom*, in May of 2017. *Frost on the Bloom* followed in November of 2017. She also writes a blog entitled "On Writing, Reading and Retirement" (www.sallyhandley.com).

An avid reader, Sally has been a mystery lover since she read her first Nancy Drew and Trixie Belden books as a young girl. An English major, she graduated from Douglass College at Rutgers University and earned her Master's Degree with a concentration in Shakespearean studies from Wroxton College, Oxfordshire, England.

After six years as a public school teacher, Sally transitioned into business, and had a 30 year career as a professional services marketer. She returned to teaching as an adjunct professor of English before retiring in 2015. Now a resident of Mauldin, SC, she devotes her time to writing cozy mysteries and gardening.

Made in United States
Orlando, FL
18 June 2023